Surf Shop Sisters

Laura Kennedy

YA Books

Published by
Fire and Ice
A Young Adult Imprint of Melange Books, LLC
White Bear Lake, MN 55110
www.fireandiceya.com

Cover Art by Caroline Andrus

To Lisa, Tracy and Jennifer, the original Surf Shop Sisters, and Lauren and Lilly, the next wave.

ACKNOWLEDGEMENTS

Thanks to my monthly "power group," composed of writers Carol J. Perry, Liz Drayer and the late Adele Woodyard, for their invaluable critiques of Brooke Bentley and her Surf Shop Sisters. Also many beau coups to the writing groups at the Tarpon Springs Library, especially David and Maria Edmonds.

No list would be complete without a special thanks to my editors at Melange Publishing, Nancy Schumacher and Caroline Andrus.

Finally, a hug and kiss to my husband Bob who has kept a roof over my head, food in the refrigerator, and ink cartridges in my printer.

Chapter One

I guess everyone wants something. It was easy figuring out what each of my three BFFs wanted at the beginning of our Junior Year at Coral Cove High. For brainy Sudsy, it was to get skinny and have a boyfriend; for gorgeous Maria, to have her parents treat her like she was older than ten; for upwardly mobile Tamara, to get more stuff.

When it came to me, all I wanted was to be taken more seriously. For some reason when you're reasonably cute, no one thinks you're very smart. Other than geometry, my grades were okay, so why was I always getting the dumb, almost-blonde treatment?

Who'd have guessed bigger problems were lurking around the bayous of Coral Cove in the form of my soon-to-be nemesis Paris Breck? But first I have to tell you about Maria and how I always seemed to get tangled up in her problems, like a clump of stinky seaweed in the Gulf of Mexico.

It was a lazy Sunday morning and I'd just glided the Green Lady (my darling convertible) through the wrought iron gates of our Mediterranean onto the brick streets to my killer job at Surf's Up. Top down, (the convertible's, not mine), I was playing a rerun of my date with Tyler the night before, wondering if being forced to defend my virginity on a weekly basis was worth the hassle of having a boyfriend.

The reggae sound of *The Expendables* met me at the door. The Sisters, aka BFFs Sudsy, Tamara and Maria, didn't seem to notice I was late. But instead of getting the evil eye from my old hippie boss, Dave, like you usually do from a grownup when you screw up, I got a sad, reassuring smile. The kind your parents give when you just broke your arm rollerblading.

I raced to a rack of bikinis and began to madly rearrange them, sneaking peeks at Sudsy and Tamara refolding a stack of Rip Curl T-shirts. Sudsy shot me a look from behind wire-rimmed Beatles glasses and shook her head. I was trying to figure out what she meant when Maria passed by carrying a box of sunblock. The crybaby of our group, tears from her big brown eyes threatened to spill down her cheeks like she was in a soap opera on Telemundo.

"What's wrong with Maria?" I whispered to Sudsy.

"She's bummed because her father told her she can't go to Homecoming with Anthony," Sudsy whispered back.

"So that's a surprise?"

"No, but she just found out Anthony will be leaving for Army boot camp after Thanksgiving. Who knows what could happen to him?"

I glanced at Maria where she stood lining up amber bottles of sunblock and gave her a little wave. But instead of a smile, she just bit her Angelina Jolie look-a-like lip.

"Leave her alone," Tamara advised. "She's just going to have to deal with it."

The morning flew by. In an attempt to pump swimwear sales, Dave coaxed me into a hot white Juicy Couture ruffled bikini (the killer suit I'd die for), to parade around the shop. I felt like an idiot, especially when two girls from school came in, but Dave was the boss.

Around one, Dave ordered a ham and pineapple pizza from Zeno's Greek Pizza Parlor. We'd just finished devouring it when a well-dressed redhead and a skinny, youngish blonde sauntered in. Sporting Kate Spade, Prada, and real jewelry, they looked like they'd be good for a couple of hundred easy. The older one, who was around fifty, reminded me of an actress I'd seen on TV reruns.

"May I help you?" I asked.

A sneer crossed the redhead's Pekinese face; the same kind of look you make when you've just spotted a big, fat cockroach.

"Tiffany wants to try on some suits. She's a seven."

"The sevens are on the rack against the wall," I said, and with a wave herded them like a sheep dog to the back.

After a few minutes of mangling the merchandise, Tiffany held up a hot turquoise T-back. "What do you think, Mommy?"

She's like thirty and still calls her mother Mommy? It was all I could do not to barf.

"Try it on. It's cute."

While Baby Cakes trotted off to the dressing room, I knocked myself out showing Mommy everything in the store. Twenty minutes later, BC reappeared with a sea foam green baby doll dress, two L-Spaces, and my to-die-for Juicy Couture bikini. She headed for the cash register, her mother trailing behind. Bingo!

"I'd kill for that suit," I said. "It's the hottest ever." Mommy handed me her American Express card and I ran it through the machine. "Paris Breck, what a pretty name. Did anyone ever tell you that you're an eponym?"

"I'm a what?" She raised one radically plucked brow.

"An eponym. When something's named after a person it's called an eponym. Of course, you're named after a person and a city too."

She looked annoyed. "Oh, really? How interesting."

"It just happens to be one of my vocabulary words from last week."

Dave high-fived me when they left. "Killer job, Brookesie. Have another piece of pizza."

"No thanks. My ass is big enough as it is."

"Your ass is perfect and you know it," Sudsy said, whisking by with the broom. But for once I wasn't worrying about the way I looked. I was worrying about Maria.

It wasn't until things slowed down and the four of us took a break at the beat up picnic table out back that we were able to talk.

"Okay, Maria, what's the scoop?" I asked.

"It's the same old thing. My dad thinks Anthony's too old and a sleezeball loser, so he won't let me date him."

Tamara wrinkled her perfectly sculptured nose. "But you do anyway, right?"

"Well, yes. But I hate sneaking around! I want to go to Homecoming and wear a pretty dress just like everyone else. It's the least I can do before he's shipped off to the Middle East." A fat tear streamed down her face.

3

I patted her hand. As usual I felt all protective and mushy. Just like in pre-school when she'd screwed up the CD player and I took the blame. "Now, don't worry, honey. We'll figure out something."

Sudsy slid a neatly typed sheet of paper to me across the table. "Well, while everyone's ruminating, here's your new vocabulary list."

I looked down. "Monday. Masticate."

"It means to chew," Sudsy explained.

"Then why the hell not just say chew?" Tamara demanded. She was not in a good mood.

Sudsy adjusted her glasses. "Because any moron can say chew, T. That's why."

Tamara rolled her eyes. "Well, it sounds like something a lot more exciting than just eating."

Sudsy and I giggled while Maria just looked bewildered.

"So why not say you're going to the dance in a group and then just sleep over at my house?" I suggested.

The Sisters nodded.

A shadow of a smile crossed Maria's face. "Do you think it will work?

"No problem. I'll run it by my mother. I'm sure she'll be okay with it."

"See, Maria, all fixed," I said. But as soon as the words left my lips I was left with a bad feeling in my stomach, like I'd just eaten a raw oyster in a month spelled without an R.

The next day at school I spent half of geometry class figuring out the logistics of my scheme to get Maria to Homecoming with Anthony by drawing little isosceles triangles on my paper. Hmm. If one corner was Maria, another Anthony, and the last corner Maria's dad.... My math teacher, Mr. Humphrey, claims side angle side equals side angle side, but in this case I had the feeling it equaled trouble.

It was Wednesday after school and I was sprawled out on an obnoxious green alligator raft in our heated pool, wondering how we were going to pull off Maria's secret date. Hopefully Maria's family would be preoccupied with making that incredible chicken with yellow rice I love, or the black bean soup I adore even more, and wouldn't notice her sneaking out her dress. My stomach growled. God, I wished I had some chicken and yellow rice.

I hopped out of the pool and wrapped myself in a huge fluffy towel. Would my mother be cooking something on that new blue European gas stove of hers, or would she just be polishing the stainless steel?

"What's for dinner?" I asked, dripping into the kitchen.

My mother blew a lock of blonde hair off her forehead. "Roast chicken with lemon, brown rice with pecans and mushrooms, and ratatouille."

"You know, I really love you."

"Yes. By the way, Sudsy called, but I didn't want to take the phone to you in the pool."

"Mom, you can't get electrocuted on a cordless phone. It runs on batteries."

"Well, it just makes me nervous." She took off her Kiss-the-Cook apron. "How's Sudsy coming with her romance novel?"

"Almost finished, but she won't let anyone read it."

"Doesn't she need someone to edit? Maybe I could help since I *am* a lit major."

"Forget it. Sudsy says it's an absolute masterpiece already."

There's an old cornball song my Grandma Donnie sings. Something about life not being easy—*I beg your pardon. I never promised you a rose garden.* I don't know who's begging whose pardon, but they were sure right about life not being a bed of flowers. I mean, I was just trying to help Maria and already I was the bad guy. At least according to Tyler.

After school the next day, Tyler and I parked the Green Lady at the Cove for the purpose of my telling him our plans had changed. Having an abundance of testosterone surging through his scrawny bod, I'm sure he thought we'd driven to the Cove to make out. So once I'd turned off the engine, I gave him a juicy kiss to get him in a good mood. Kissing Tyler was really quite delicious, because, scrawny or not, he was one of the hottest guys at Coral Cove High. But when I pushed him away and blurted out that he'd have to meet me at Homecoming because I'd be

5

going to the dance in a group date with Sudsy, Tamara, and Maria, he was not happy.

"But I thought Maria was going with that Anthony dude?"

"She is. But her father can't stand him, so she has to pretend she's going with us girls and then sleep over at my house."

"You must be friggin' kidding," he croaked. Sometimes when Tyler gets excited his voice still goes up and down like the Scorpion ride at Busch Gardens.

"No, I'm not kidding, Tyler. This dance is like extremely crucial to Maria. I can't let her down."

"But it's all right to let me down."

"I don't see what the big deal is. We can still be at the dance together."

"So does that mean we won't be hanging out after?"

I looked at him and smiled, realizing that hanging out meant making out in the back seat of my convertible.

"There'll be plenty of other times for that. Think of it this way. Helping Anthony and Maria go to Homecoming is sort of like your patriotic duty. I mean, Anthony could get killed when he's in the army. It's the least you can do."

A scowl crossed his handsome face. "You know, Brooke, I'm really sick of the way you always manipulate me."

"With the exception of now, when have I manipulated you?"

"All the time. You constantly have some kind of scheme."

"Tyler, that's not true. Besides, in business they call that entrepreneurship."

"Right."

We drove back to school in silence; Tyler turned away from me like my cat does on the way home from the vet. I stopped at the bike rack where he got out of the Green Lady and slammed the door.

"You don't have to take it out on my car," I said.

He turned and glared. "I wish you worried half as much about me as you do about your damn car. Well, you won't have to worry about it anymore."

"So does that meaning you're breaking up with me?"

"What do you think?" he snapped and with that unlocked his bike and pedaled off in a cloud of dust.

Chapter Two

There seems to be some kind of an irony in this universe that when you want a great day to come it never does. But when you dread some big disaster of a day it's here before you know it. That's how it was with Friday's Homecoming, a date I'd circled on my calendar in red. Totally bummed out about Tyler and my life in general, Homecoming crept closer and closer, like a deadly virus.

At seven o'clock that Friday night, I tiptoed down our staircase in my lime green strapless dress, three-inch strappy heels, and my best going-to-homecoming-dance expression.

My mother stood at the foot of the stairs, obsessively misting pots of white orchids. She stopped mid-mist. "Honey, you're absolutely gorgeous! Let me look at you."

I leaned against the wrought iron railing to pose.

"Bud, come and see how beautiful Brooke looks," she called. "And bring the camera." I froze on the stairs, waiting for my father to record another Hallmark moment. The smile on my mother's face dissolved. "But Tyler isn't here yet."

"Mom, I'm not going to Homecoming with Tyler. We broke up."

"You broke up?" Her face was incredulous.

I nodded. "I really don't want to talk about it right now, but sometimes you have to sacrifice for the nobler cause."

My mother gave me a blank look.

"The Sisters and I are going in a group. Besides, one on one boy-girl isn't really that in anymore."

"It's not?"

My father and little brother Benji appeared around the corner just in time to hear my last sentence. My father looked alarmed. "I hope you're not getting any funny ideas about girls."

"No, don't worry. I'm not gay."

"Oh, I wasn't saying that," my father said. He looked flustered. "I just thought it was kind of weird..."

Benji snorted. "They go in groups because they can't get dates."

"Now, Benji, Brooke has never had a problem attracting boys. Of course, neither did I." My mother looked wistful. "When I was in high school it was all about who was asked or wasn't asked to a dance. My best friend Katie spent the entire night of the prom locked in her room crying and stuffing chocolate donuts."

"How sad," I said. How utterly dumb, I thought.

"Don't worry, Dad. You don't have to take me. Once Maria gets here, we're going together in the Green Lady. We're meeting Sudsy and Tamara there."

I had no more than mentioned her name than the doorbell rang. My mother opened the door on cue. There stood Maria on the porch, dressed in blue jean shorts and a T-shirt, her plastic covered formal over her arm.

"Maria, honey, you're not dressed yet?" my mother said, letting her in.

"I thought I'd get dressed here, Mrs. Bentley," she answered, a guilty look crossing her gorgeous face. "I didn't want to wrinkle my formal."

"Won't it get wrinkled on the way over to school?" Benji asked, appearing around the corner, a huge flirty grin on his face. At twelve, my brother had been crazy about Maria since he could crawl.

Maria and I raced upstairs to my room so she could change. "We have to hurry or we'll be late," I said, removing her yellow formal from the plastic once I closed my bedroom door. "You know how impatient Tamara is."

Maria bit her lip lower lip in that aggravatingly attractive way she had. "I told Anthony to meet us in the parking lot."

"Good idea." Maria pulled off her shorts and T-shirt and slipped into the wisp of yellow fabric. I zipped up her up and she stepped into her gold heels.

9

"There," I said. "We're ready."

"Ready," Maria echoed as she took my hand. We stood side-by-side staring at our reflections in my floor length mirror. The soft fabric of Maria's strapless dress clung to her in a way I could only dream it could on me.

"You look like a piece of Greek lemon cake at Hellas' bakery," I said.

Maria squeezed my hand. "Oh, Boo, you are the best friend ever." Tears threatened to spill from her doe-like eyes.

"Now, don't cry. You'll run your mascara."

A cell phone rang. From the look on Maria's face when she answered, I knew it had to be Anthony. "Yes, I'm ready," she whispered. "I'll meet you in front of the school in ten minutes." She hung up. "Brooke, I'm so scared."

"Stop worrying. Your parents will never know."

We drove to Coral Cove High, Maria busy texting Sudsy and Tamara that we were on our way. When she was through, she popped one pink fingernail into her mouth.

"Now don't start chewing off your nail polish," I warned, reminding me of the way I used to tell her not to suck her thumb in kindergarten. "Everything is going to be just fine."

Dear God, Please help us get through this without Maria's parents finding out and I promise I will be a better person. I will start that recycling program at school I promised the last time I prayed for something. And I will be nicer to my little brother.

The way they always tell it in novels, everything was fine until the end. Maria and I met Anthony outside of school in the parking lot, catching Sudsy, Tamara and Tamara's boyfriend, Jamal, inside the gym. And even though Tyler and I glared at each other off and on all night, everything went according to plan.

That is, everything went according to plan until Homecoming was over and Sudsy and I, minus Maria, pulled through the wrought iron gates leading to my Mediterranean and spotted a black Lincoln Town Car in the driveway.

"Isn't that Maria's father's car?" Sudsy asked.

"Ohmigod!" I said. "It is his car!"

Sudsy gasped. "It looks like a hearse."

"Well, as strict as Maria's parents are, it may as well be."

I pulled the Green Lady into the garage and Sudsy and I tiptoed through the kitchen.

"Brooke, is that you?" My mother's voice floated around the corner. "We have some visitors."

If I could just disappear. Or if something would happen to divert everyone's attention, like maybe a hurricane. But it was the end of September. Hurricane season was over. Maria's parents stood in the living room, their stone-like faces like the carvings of the presidents on Mount Rushmore.

I forced my face into a smile. "Hi," I said. "So nice to see you again."

My father's thundercloud expression told me he was mega mad. "Okay, young lady, tell me what's going on?" Where's Maria?"

It was over. Done. Kaput. I was toast. I closed my traitorous blue eyes. I'd only been trying to help my friend and now I was in way more trouble than I could ever remember being in.

"Well," I began, choosing my words like I was buying donuts at the bakery at Publix. "It's like this: Maria had her heart set on going to the Homecoming dance…" and out came the entire pathetic saga.

"She sneaked out. I knew it." Maria's father was Mount Vesuvius just boiled over. "She disobeyed her father and disrespected her family. And you helped her."

Maria's mother waved her hand. "Now, amor, don't be too hard on Brooke. I'm sure Maria put her up to it. No?"

My mother bit her lip. "Mr. Martinez, I'm afraid Brooke is very much a part of this and we're very sorry. As I told you, her father and I were aware of nothing. All we knew was that the girls were having a sleepover here after the dance."

I looked up to see Benji spying over the upstairs railing.

"Okay, so where is Maria?" my father thundered. From the way he acted, you'd think we'd just robbed a bank or something.

Everyone glared at me. Even Sudsy looked disapproving.

It was like watching one of those old *I Love Lucy* reruns on TV where Lucy tries to talk herself out of some mess. Come to think of it, Mr. Martinez reminded me of Ricky Ricardo. I scrutinized his face. He and Desi Arnez were about the same height and age. Desi was better looking, but there was certainly—

"Brooke?" My mother sat down beside me. "What's this all about? I thought you girls were going to the dance in a group?"

I shook my head to come out of my daze. "Well, like I was saying, Maria wanted to go to Homecoming with Anthony because he's like going in the Army next month and they, like, you know, want to spend—"

"Anthony?" Mr. Martinez bellowed. "That diablo! He is not only Greek, he is a sneak and a liar!" He looked strangely pale.

Maria's mother put her finger to her mouth and shushed. "Jorge, callate. Now Brooke, go on."

"So Jamal and Anthony met us at the dance and..."

"So you mean that Maria and Anthony are *together* now?" From the way Mrs. Martinez said *together,* I knew she could only be thinking one thing.

"Well, I guess." Of course, I knew they were at the Cove making out as we spoke. I only hoped Anthony wouldn't talk innocent Maria into going too far.

My mother said something.

"What?" I mewed.

"I said, don't you think you owe Maria's parents an apology?"

I looked at Maria's parents. "I'm really sorry, Mr. and Mrs. Martinez," I began. "I just wanted to help. The whole idea was mine, so please don't be too mad at Maria."

Just then the doorbell rang. My mother got up to answer it, returning with Maria, a scared looking Cinderella returning from the ball. Fervently, I wished I were somewhere else. Anywhere. The adults all looked at each other as though they were trying to decide just who would chew Maria out first. Fortunately, my parents are Scandinavian so they don't yell a lot. I looked at Maria's father, waiting for him to explode again. But sometimes words aren't necessary, even if you are Hispanic. Maria looked at her parents and began to cry.

Mr. Martinez pointed toward our front door. "Home, Maria," he said. "Now."

Blinking back tears, Maria practically ran to the front door, her parents sprinting behind. The door slammed and Sudsy, my parents, and I were alone.

"Bed," my father said. *Succinct,* I thought, recalling an old vocab word. It's so nice when words fit.

Sudsy's face had turned as red as her rose colored dress. "Mrs. Bentley, maybe I should just go home," she suggested in a whisper. "I'll call my father."

My mother shook her head. "No, I want you to stay, Sophia. There is no need to alarm your parents at this time of night."

Sudsy nodded and we limped out of the living room, two wilted flowers.

How did things get so screwed up? I wondered as we climbed the stairs to my bedroom. *Why did stuff like this always happen to me?*

I couldn't remember ever feeling so miserable. Do they let sixteen-year-old girls join the convent? At least I could spend my inevitable mega-week restriction where it was quiet. Forget the fact I wasn't even Catholic. Maybe the Pope would feel sorry for me and make a special dispensation since I'd had such good intentions. But deep down I knew there'd be no intervention, divine or otherwise.

Benji peeked out of his bedroom door as we crept by, his face a comic strip question mark. He gave a little wave as I staggered into my room.

Well, even though I was in trouble, Maria had gone to Homecoming with the boy she loved. As for me, I didn't have a boyfriend any more. Another good reason to join a convent.

"I hope that Maria's parents don't go too ballistic punishing her," Sudsy whispered.

"I don't think they're sadistic or anything. They probably just won't let her out of the house forever."

Emotionally exhausted, Sudsy and I crawled into bed. I was just turning off the light when I thought about checking my text messages. There were two; one from Tamara and one from Maria.

I opened Tamara's first.

Skipping sleepover. Heard you and Maria were busted. T.

Exhausted, I forced my fingers to type these few simple words— *true that…totally busted.*

I opened Maria's next, expecting an emotionally draining novella. Surprisingly, her message was short. *Sorry Boo, love M*

Sleep is a wonderful thing. It's like the best escape. I'd read that in Mexico you can go to this place where they give you a shot and you can sleep for two weeks. I could sleep through my whole restriction. What a killer idea.

I hugged my pillow. I love you, I thought deliriously. You are my only friend. My parents hate me. Maria's parents hate me. Tyler hates me. I flipped my tear dampened pillow and fell asleep.

In spite of the hideous state of my life, the sun came up like usual the next morning. Slices of sunlight crept through the plantation shutters. I glanced at the clock. Twenty after nine. I turned to the spot where Sudsy slept only to find it empty. Obviously she'd skipped out early.

Good idea. I wish I had someplace to run to.

Stumbling across the floor, I opened the double shutters overlooking the backyard. One squeal and I knew Benji was already in the pool. I stared at him and his friend, Kyle, flaying around. *Oh God, to be twelve again.* What bliss. No worries. No restriction. No boyfriends. Okay, so for Benji and Kyle, no girlfriends. Just splashing aimlessly in the pool, hitting your best friend with a foam rubber Snoodle.

A creature of habit, I glanced at my nightstand for my vocab list. As if it mattered if I *had* a good vocabulary. I mean, I only wanted to learn new words so I could be respected for my intellect. Fat chance of being respected for anything now. The whole school would know about the Maria fiasco by Monday. I looked at my word for the day. *Saturday— Ennui—listlessness, dissatisfaction, boredom.* How apropos.

Chapter Three

I crept downstairs. From years of experience, I've found it best to keep a low profile when on the big G, aka being grounded. Miraculously, no one was in the kitchen. If I were a bookie, I would have bet my entire fortune ($134.58 accruing at half-a-percent per annum at SunTrust Bank) that my father was golfing. I already knew Benji was in the pool. And my mother?

I was foraging in the cupboard for hi-protein powder when that Nancy Drew mystery was solved and my mother popped around the corner. As usual she looked cuter than a mother should be allowed.

"Hi, honey. Glad you're up," she said. She pushed a wisp of blonde hair out of her eyes. "I'm going to have breakfast at The Green Iguana with the girls. By the way, your father and I agreed on a two-week restriction."

I nodded my head like a trained Shetland.

"That means no mall, no movies, no Tyler. Oh, I forgot you broke up. And by the way, that means no driving the Green Lady."

"No driving?"

"Your father's idea. He took the keys. Both sets. Now please keep an eye on Benji and Kyle in the pool. I know they swim like fish, but they're only twelve. I'll be back in a couple of hours. Thanks." She kissed my forehead, and breezed out the door to the garage.

Oh great. My parents *were* really sick. They'd taken away the one thing I loved best in the entire world— my car. How could I get around? I still had to go to school and work. And then it hit me. *Work.*

"But I have to be at Surf's Up at twelve-thirty."

"I'll be back by noon to give you a ride. Promise."

15

My life sucks. I was sprawled out in a lounge chair multi-tasking, i.e. life guarding Benji and Kyle in the pool and expressing my life sucks sentiment in a text to Tamara, when my cell rang. It was T.

"Okay, Brooke, I need the entire scoop. *Totally busted* just doesn't do it."

"Have you talked to Maria?" I asked, wanting to avoid the recitation of the previous night's debacle.

"No. I called, but her father answered and said 'Maria no longer may talk on the phone.' You think she'd stolen the Mona Lisa or something."

"I know."

"Okay, so spill it."

"Well," I began tentatively, "it was like this." Two minutes later, guts spilled, I sank back in the lounge chair in a state of total exhaustion.

"Damn." For once Tamara was practically speechless.

"I second that." I took a deep breath and attempted to change the subject. "Are you working today?"

"I wasn't, but Dave called and asked me to fill in for Maria. Her parents won't let her work while she's grounded."

"And how long is that?"

"A month."

"Double damn."

Lifeguard duty over, I escaped to the garage to pump air into the tires of my beach cruiser. It wasn't long before my mother pulled up in her turquoise Corvette. She hadn't forgotten me after all. After fishing the still-wet boys off the couch, she made them sandwiches and Kyle went home. Warning Benji to behave himself, we took off for work. She chattered all the way, just like everything was okay. I made her drop me off half-a-block from Surf's Up. Like, who wants to be seen chauffeured around by their mother, even if she does drive a Corvette? I mean, how much humiliation can a girl take?

The sound of Bob Marley's reggae filled the air. Dave was busy waxing a surfboard when I dragged in. He smiled when he saw me. I returned the smile, grateful he was an old hippie.

"Rough night, huh?" he said.

"Totally."

"Achein'. Sometimes it's a bummer getting slammed when you're only trying to help a bud."

"How did you know?"

"Tamara told me. I'd already figured Maria was in love. I was in love once."

"You were?"

"Yeah. Of course, I've had a lot of other girlfriends."

"Of course."

"But for me, there was only one woman. I met her at Woodstock in August of '69."

"Woodstock?"

He nodded. There was a faraway look in his eyes. "Yeah, the three most wonderful days of my life."

I pictured Dave, young, no wrinkles and grey hair, dancing in the mud, getting high, making love.

"What was she like?"

"Beautiful. Long blonde hair, blue eyes. The coolest girl I ever met. I never saw her again."

"Never saw her?" I sounded like a parrot, but I couldn't help it.

"I lost her phone number." A tear slipped down Dave's lined face onto the board. He rubbed the drop away with the tip of his bony finger. "I tried to find her, but I couldn't remember her name. I think it was Denise something."

"Oh, Dave, I'm so sorry."

Embarrassed, I patted his shoulder. The pain in my chest was like my heart splitting in two. How awful! To love someone your entire life and not even know where she was. It was more than I could imagine, because even though Tyler and I had broken up, there was always a chance we'd get back together. Does a broken heart really last forever? It was a scary thought.

The afternoon dragged by. With only Tamara and me working, things were dull as Grandma Donnie's cooking. No intellectual remarks from Sudsy. No wistful remarks from Maria. Just work, work, work.

"I suppose your parents expect you home right away," Tamara said. We were out back at the picnic table, drinking Dr. Pepper and stuffing Fritos.

17

"What do you think?" I growled. "It's my first day of restriction." I tossed a Frito across the table at Tamara. "No good deed goes unpunished."

"True, but you were the one who thought of the sleepover."

"Well, it sounded like a good idea at the time."

We sat eating and drinking until Tamara gave a loud Dr. Pepper burp. "Well, I'm sorry."

"For burping or me being on restriction?"

"Both. I'd give you a ride home, but I'm riding my bike. Good exercise and all that."

"That's okay, T. A walk will do me good."

The distance from Surf's Up to Porpoise Drive was fifteen minutes max. No big deal.

I took a shortcut through Sawgrass Park where I sauntered to the lake to look for alligators from the boardwalk. I spotted a baby sunning himself on the bank. He looked up with his binocular-size eyes and swam my way.

"I'm sorry," I said, "but I don't have anything to feed you. It's against the law. Can't you read the sign? *Do Not Molest the Alligators.*"

He gave me a questioning look.

"I mean, aren't I in enough trouble already? Besides, you caught me at a bad time. I am foodless, boyfriendless, and hopeless." And with that confession, I sat down on the bench and began to cry. Darn it. I hadn't shed a tear over this whole thing, but here I was Miss Cry Baby. Wah, wah, wah. Thank God no one was around to see me except a baby gator. I cried some more. Not like hysterical or anything, just a quiet little cathartic cry. I wiped away a tear and got up.

I was just crossing the parking lot, when a pink Cadillac pulled in and parked. There was a popping noise and the trunk flew open. A woman got out of the driver's side, followed by a woman who got out of the other. They looked awfully familiar. Blonde, attractive and Botoxed. Then it hit me. It was Paris Breck, the Eponym Lady, and her daughter, Tiffany. Except last week Paris had red hair. I was nearing the Caddy when a tiny, beige shih Tzu jumped from Tiffany's arms and tore across the parking lot.

"Omigod," Tiffany screamed. "Tutu got away! Come back, you little shit. Alyse, do something!"

I turned, looking to see if someone else had shown up, but saw no one.

"You, over there," Tiffany caterwauled. "Don't just stand there! Catch her!"

Startled, I lunged for the dog as she shot past. "Stop, you little brat. Stop this nonsense right now!"

The agitated ball of fluff stopped and did a one-eighty. "Now, that's better." I knelt down and picked her up. "Alligators eat little dogs like you for snacks, you know. It's not very pleasant to think about, but it's reality."

Tutu licked my face. When I looked up, Paris and Tiffany were standing in front of me.

"Oh, thank you!" Blonde wig askew, Paris held out her arms for the delinquent dog. "I don't know what possessed her."

"I recognize you," Tiffany said. "You waited on us the other day at Surf's Up."

Paris' distraught look morphed into a smile. "Yes, you're the quirky girl who said I was a…"

"An eponym," I answered.

"You also said you adored the Juicy Couture bikini I bought," Tiffany added.

"Adored is an understatement. I'd do anything for that suit."

Paris laughed. "Well, we all have our price, don't we?"

We turned back to the Pepto Bismol pink Caddy. "Tell me," Paris asked, "do you always walk through the park?"

"No. I have a car, but unfortunately my parents took away the keys for two weeks."

"So, that's why you look so bummed," Tiffany said. "Here, maybe this will cheer you up." She reached into the open trunk of the car and pulled out a Dillard's shopping bag. "I want you to have this," she said and handed me an adorable Marilyn Monroe clutch purse. "As a reward for catching Tutu."

"Omigod! A Betsey Johnson. I couldn't."

Laura Kennedy

"Nonsense," Paris interrupted. "Of course you can. Besides, it cost practically nothing."

Chapter Four

I spent the rest of the way home admiring my new Betsey Johnson clutch. It was absolutely killer. I'd carry it to school Monday when I wore my black parachute pants and white blouse. I guess Paris and Tiffany were pretty nice after all, despite the fact their makeup looked like it had been put on with a trowel. Well, as Mrs. Ethos always says, you can't tell a book by its dust jacket.

Restriction Evening Number One (and who's counting?) was spent in the old Mediterranean familial nest; my mother in the living room sprawled on the couch reading something for her Latin American Lit class; my dad and Benji watching a gross reality show where they make you eat spiders; and me in my room.

Around eight o'clock I came down for some Haagen-Dazs. I passed by my reclining mother and glanced at the novel she was reading. *One Hundred Years of Solitude*. Unreal. I could hardly handle one night.

Benji and I met at the freezer. Fortunately, he was after a Nestle Crunch ice cream bar, because I was not up to a food fight.

"You don't look very happy," he said as he tore the wrapper off his favorite treat.

"I'm not. I'm suffering from ennui."

"Is it catching?"

"No. It's mainly a female thing."

I grabbed the pint of Haagen-Dazs and a spoon and headed toward the stairs. Why should I care if ice cream had a zillion calories and I would probably end up looking like I was wearing a fat suit? Besides, weren't adults always telling us looks don't count? I trotted through the living room. My mom pushed her glasses onto her forehead.

21

"Hungry?

"No, just bored. Sorry, I forgot mango is your fav too."

She smiled. "That's okay. I'm drinking a spinach/celery cocktail."

I looked at her teeth. "I can tell. How's the book?"

"Great. Gabriel Garcia Marquez is incredible." She paused. "I'm sorry about this restriction, but…"

"I know. I deserve it."

She nodded and put the glasses back on. "It will be over before you know it."

"Right."

I passed my cat, Erskine, on the stairs. He must have smelled the mango ice cream, because he rubbed against my leg and purred.

"You're such a sycophant, Erskine. You really are. The second I saw the word on my vocabulary list I thought of you."

Erskine gave a plaintive meow.

"Okay, maybe not the exact second, but you have to admit the only time you're the least bit nice is when you want something." I climbed the stairs to my cell, Erskine at my heels.

It's a funny thing about being on restriction. I mean, when it's a Saturday night and you're not at Movieco or Starbucks drinking a Vanilla Latte, but are stuck at home, there really isn't much to do except your homework. I settled down with the pint of Haagen-Dazs, my cat, and my English Comp assignment.

In a minimum of 500 words, write about a recent memorable experience telling what you may or may not have learned. Do so in a creative manner.

"What do you think, Erskine? Does Mrs. Ethos really want to hear about my most recent memorable experience?"

I paused. "Does that meow mean *yes,* or that you want more ice cream?"

I scooped the last of the melting dessert into the carton lid and placed it on the floor, then opened my laptop and logged on. Five hundred words, I thought, arranging myself cross-legged on the bed. Well, if Jane Austen could write a gazillion words with a turkey quill, I should be able to manage five hundred words on a PC. I stared at the blank screen. The cursor flashed at me ominously as though asking, "Okay, Brooke, spill your guts."

Five pages later I was through. Totally exhausted, I hit spell check, zipped through the corrections. How Jane A. did it, I didn't know. Maybe she was on restriction too. I mean, they probably made her milk the cows or something, but the bottom line was her parents probably wouldn't let her the hell out of the house either.

I flicked off the computer, washed my face and brushed my sugarcoated-teeth. I lay there worrying. Everyone would know about the Maria caper at school. The worst part of it all was losing Tyler. But I wasn't going to call him. I had my pride.

Monday, Monday. The line from Grandma Donnie's old Mamas and Papas album leapfrogged through my head. Why couldn't they just get rid of Monday mornings altogether? And as long as I was wishing, I may as well wish I wasn't sixteen. Why couldn't I be old, like twenty or something?

I was hiding under my duvet, planning how I could stay home sick, when my mother appeared. I peeked out from under the covers. Behind her was Benji.

"Brooke, why aren't you up?" She was dressed in yellow, her hair swept up in an interesting cockatoo look.

"I don't feel so good."

There was a moment of silence. It was obvious she was deciding if I was sick or simply (recent vocab word) incorrigible.

"She really is sick, Mom," Benji offered. "She's got ennui."

A smile snuck around the corners of my mother's mouth.

"Well, a little ennui never hurt anyone, Benji. As for you, Brooke, I expect you downstairs, dressed and ready to be driven to school in ten minutes. And I mean it."

Any other time if you'd asked me how I like school, I'd say it was okay. I mean, sometimes classes are a drag, but some of the teachers are really nice and try to make stuff interesting. The most important thing about school is that it's the backdrop for my social life. Like, where my friends and my boyfriend are or I should say, was. It's where I try out

23

new outfits, find out the skinny about who's dating who, and who broke up over the weekend.

Prisons have a killer grapevine, no pun intended. But compared to the grapevine at Coral Cove, it's probably the Pony Express versus Fed Ex. I barely had one Rainbow flip-flop through the front door before I heard the whispering.

Brooke—Homecoming dance—Maria-Tyler. Whisper, whisper, whisper.

I shot a lethal look at Chief Gossip Girl and cheerleader, Logan Lee. She was holding court with some of the most popular girls in school.

I remained cool as the Antarctic as I sailed by. That is, until I looked up to see Tyler meandering down the hall with who of all people but Paige Barton! And, he was holding her hand! My head spun around like the girl in the *Exorcist.* What? Tyler and Paige? And I thought she was one of my best second-tier friends.

The Surf Shop Sisters were waiting for me at my locker, sad little smiles pasted on their faces.

"Hi," Sudsy said.

I plunked my books on the floor and spun the dial on my lock. "Hi."

"We just wanted to be here for you," Maria began, "because we know you're bummed."

Sudsy patted my shoulder. "We were by the trophy case when you saw Tyler with Paige."

"Yeah," Tamara said. "But you might feel a lot better about the situation when I pop that skinny little honky in the eye."

"Thanks, T, but no violence." I slammed my locker door. "Besides, I was the one who jilted Tyler. He felt cuckolded."

"Cuckolded?" Maria repeated.

"Cheated on," Sudsy explained. "Except, it was with a girl and there was no sex."

"It's my fault, Boo." Maria looked ready to cry.

"Maria, I'm not blaming you. Please don't get emotional."

But the truth was, I *did* blame her, at least a little. Sure, the Maria sleepover was my idea, and we were both on, but Maria *still* had a boyfriend.

I picked up my books. "Got to go. See you guys at lunch."

I struggled through the day. By last period English Comp, I was whipped. I dragged by Mrs. Ethos's desk and deposited my composition in her homework basket. She looked up from her attendance printout and smiled. "Well, aren't we diligent? This assignment isn't due until tomorrow."

"I know. I just thought I'd be early for a change."

The next fifty minutes dragged by as Mrs. Ethos attempted to explain the difference between a past tense and a past-progressive tense until I was feeling pretty tense myself. I glanced down at my gnawed nail polish. *Brooke, if you don't mellow out, you will have no fingers left.* I was stuffing my grammar book into my backpack when I looked up to see Mrs. Ethos peering at me from behind her desk.

"Would you mind staying a minute? I'd like to talk to you."

Oh, great. Don't tell me she's heard about the Maria sleepover too. I crept toward the front of the room.

"Yes?" My voice was barely a chirp.

"While the class was working, I read your composition *What I Learned Last Weekend*." She pulled my composition from under a big glass seagull paperweight. "I thought it was quite good."

"You did?"

She nodded. "You wrote with a combination of honesty and humor that was quite poignant. I especially liked your analogy to *Don Quixote* about being naïve." She held my theme out to me.

I took the sheet of paper from her hand. On the top right hand corner was a large red A+. For a brief second I was almost happy. "Thank you, Mrs. Ethos. I don't know what to say."

"You deserve it, Brooke. By the way, I was wondering if you'd be interested in competing in this year's Senior High Vocabulary Bee?"

"Vocabulary Bee?"

"It's like a spelling bee, except contestants define words. As head of the English Department, it's my job to pick two students from Coral

25

Cove to compete in the West Florida Competition. It will be held in Tampa the first weekend of December. Unfortunately, one of my original picks is moving out of the area."

"Don't you have any other students who are, like, smarter?"

She laughed. "Brooke, you underestimate yourself. You are very bright. You just don't know it."

She paused while I digested this revelation. "Could you possibly take the qualifying quiz now?

"Well, I don't know. I'm kinda stressed."

"I realize you're at a disadvantage, but I must have the names of the two students by four o'clock this afternoon." She handed me the quiz and a number-two pencil. "There are twenty-six questions and twenty-six answers. Place the alphabetical letter of the definition next to the word that is to be defined. Now, don't turn the page until I say go."

I sat in my seat, wrote my name at the top of the answer sheet, and took a deep breath.

"Ready?" she asked.

"Ready," I answered.

"Go."

Number 1. *Avaricious.* Easy. Wasn't that what Sudsy was always calling Tamara?

From then on I went into kind of a trance. A trance of words dancing through my brain. Amazingly, half of them were from Sudsy's list. It seemed like the only word they forgot was cuckold. When I was through, I quickly checked my answers.

"I'm through, Mrs. Ethos."

"Are you sure, Brooke? You have three more minutes."

"I'm sure."

While Mrs. Ethos graded my quiz, I gnawed the end of my number-two pencil. I know it was school property and all that, but my nerves were shot.

After a few minutes, she looked up. "Congratulations. You scored twenty-three out of twenty-six answers. And that means you'll be representing Coral Cove High."

I practically levitated (yesterday's vocab word) out of the room. Me representing Coral Cove in the Vocabulary Bee! Unreal. And Mrs. Ethos said I was smart. I couldn't remember anyone ever telling me that. Smart ass, yes. Adorable, hot, but never intelligent. I could hardly wait to tell Sudsy.

Sudsy was already at our special lunch table devouring a huge gyro when I slid my composition down next to her.

"Shut up! A+? You got a friggin' A+?"

"Mrs. Ethos said she was impressed with my honesty and humor, and that I was quite *poignant.* Thanks to you, I even knew what she meant."

"I am so proud of you, Brooke. I feel like Mia's grandmother in the *Princess Diaries.*"

"And get this, I'm going to be in the Vocabulary Bee competition. I took the test and practically all the words you gave me were on it."

"Omigod!"

"I wonder who the other person is?" Tamara said.

I looked up to see Tamara and Maria who'd just plunked down at the table.

I looked at Sudsy. "You?"

"No. I'm disqualified because I went last year. I think it might be Chad Roshbaum."

Tamara made a face. "The tall geeky guy who carries a briefcase?"

"He's the dude," Sudsy answered.

"That is one square white boy. Maybe you two can hook up, Brooke."

"No thanks, T."

Maria stuck out her famous Angelina Jolie lip. "Hey, that's not nice. Chad is really very sweet. He helps me with my algebra."

"Yeah, and I bet he'd like to help you with something else." Tamara laughed. "Would you date him?"

"I might if I didn't have Anthony."

Sudsy threw a Frito at Maria. "Liar."

"That's wonderful about the competition, Brooke," Maria said, changing the subject. "I could never be as smart as you all are."

Tamara poked a finger into one of Maria's Grand Canyon dimples. "Girl, the way you look, you don't have to worry about being smart."

27

Sudsy straightened and I knew we were in for lecture number twenty-two. "Tamara, that's *exactly* the wrong message to send Maria. Women have to learn to not depend on their looks. They must be educated, confident independent individuals who can take care of themselves. Remember, beauty fades."

Tamara did one of her shoulder rolls. "Suds, have you ever seen Maria's mother?"

"Well, yes. She *is* still pretty. But remember, I've seen her abuelita, too."

It was after school and I was walking past the bike racks in the parking lot when I spotted Tyler. He was alone. When he saw me, he looked like he wanted to run. Instead, he gave a feeble wave.

"Hi."

"Hi, yourself."

There was a long pause while he unlocked his bike. He looked up and our eyes met.

"It didn't take you long to find another girlfriend." My words were like poison darts.

Tyler snorted. "Paige isn't my girlfriend. We're, like, friends."

"Friends who hold hands? How sweet."

"Damn it, Brooke. You and I planned on Homecoming for weeks. I even got a friggin' suit and paid for it myself."

I winced. "I'm sorry, Tyler. About the suit, I mean."

"It's not just that I had to bag a hell of a lot groceries at Publix to get the friggin' money. It's that you don't care. Your friends are more important to you than I am."

He jumped on his bike. I watched him pedal away, my anger dissolving like a sugar lump in a mug of steamy Vanilla Latte. Tyler was right. It *was* all my fault. I'd basically stood him up so Maria could go to the Homecoming Dance with Anthony. I'd traded Tyler's love for Maria's friendship. And now I'd lost him for good. A tear hit my nose and dove down my cheek.

I turned and headed in the direction of Porpoise Drive, moving about as fast as the sand turtle that lives under our deck. Why hurry? I had nothing to look forward to. Absolutely nothing except the

Vocabulary Bee. Somehow the idea of spending the next two weeks curled up with Webster's Dictionary made me want to cry even more.

Chapter Five

When life really sucks i.e., your parents are virtually through with you, it's nice to have a grandparent or two. They love you no matter what. And God only knows, that's what I needed. I punched the almost forgotten number into my cell.

"Brooke?" Grandma Donnie said. "Is it actually you?"

Guilt shot down to my Rainbows. "Yeah. Thought I'd call to say hi."

"Well, hi to you."

"And, I just wanted to tell you how much I appreciate all your unconditional love." There was silence while she digested this bit of bull.

She laughed. "Well, thanks. Where are you, anyway?"

"At Spring Bayou by the clubhouse. I'm really bored and don't have anything to do."

"I'll be there in ten minutes."

I was perched on a park bench texting the Sisters when Grandma Donnie pulled into the parking lot in her red Mercedes SL. She wore huge Hollywood sunglasses and a red pantsuit. Around her neck hung a gold chain that would have made Elvis jealous.

"Hi, Hot Shot," she said when I ambled over to the car. "Get in."

"I better call Mom. I'm sort of like on restriction."

"I gathered. I phoned her on the way over."

I settled into the butter-soft leather seat. "Did she tell you the mall is strictly verboten?"

"Yes, and she's made an exception as long as I swear not to buy you anything. We *are* doing lunch, though. They still allow you to eat, don't they?"

Cruising with my hyper grandma through the mall was like playing elf helper to Mrs. Claus on diet pills. And, I mean, who but my grandmother would wear a tight red pantsuit in eighty-degree heat? And who would talk non-stop to complete strangers about the unbelievable sale on Stuart Weitzman shoes?

After a half-hour beauty excursion to the Lancôme counter at Dillard's, we were ready for food. It wasn't until dessert that I was up to recapping Friday night and the entire Maria debacle.

"And that's how it was," I said, after taking my last bite of crème brule.

"So you threw yourself under the bus so your girlfriend could go to the dance with the love of her life."

"Something like that."

She admired a perfectly manicured nail. "Well, I think you're very noble, Brooke."

"You do?"

"Yes. Incredibly insane, but noble."

"Thanks. I wish my parents thought the same thing."

"Sometimes parents forget what it's like to be in love."

I looked into Donnie's eyes. There was a softness I'd never seen. She laughed. "You never knew your Donnie was in love?"

"Well, I never, you know, thought about it."

"Well, I was. Deliriously, wildly in love. With your grandfather."

"But I thought he took off when Mom was a baby?"

"He did. But that didn't mean I didn't love Dean."

"Dean?"

"A surfer boy from California I met at Woodstock. Tall and blonde with green eyes and a space between his teeth."

"Woodstock?"

She nodded. "It was August 1969 and there were more people on that farm than I'd ever seen in one place. We were hungry, and high, and soaking wet from the rain. But it was all absolutely wonderful. Just love, love, love."

I gulped.

She dabbed at her eyes with a napkin. "But for Dean and me we felt totally alone." Donnie reached for the check and her Donald Pliner

31

purse. "Well, enough nostalgia."

I smiled, but under the table I was counting on my fingers. If the infamous Woodstock concert was in August 1969, and my mom was born on May 17th the following year—Omigod! It hit me like a ten-pound grouper. Grandma Donnie got knocked up at Woodstock! Not only that, Dave met the love of *his* life at Woodstock. Could it be possible? No, not Dave. He couldn't be my *grandfather!* The idea was too totally bizarre for words.

I could hardly wait to tell the Sisters my theory the next day at school, but a Sister lunch was not in my future. T was practicing for track, Sudsy was doing lunch with the yearbook staff, and Maria was in the library finishing her English Lit assignment. Which left me alone with my suspicions about Dave.

Thank God for Surf's Up. We were all there when school was over, even Maria, whose parents had capitulated (i.e. given in) about the no work thing. I saw Sudsy and winked, motioning her to where I was dusting surfboards. She shook her head and pointed to Dave on his campstool behind the cash register. I sidled by Tamara pricing sunblock with a big sticker gun, and winked again.

"Girl, what's going on with your eyes?"

"T, my eyes are fine," I whispered. "I just want to tell you something."

"Well, it better be good, because Flower Child is feeling his boss thing today."

"I think I know who my grandfather is."

"Yeah, so you don't think it's Elvis anymore?"

"No. Someone more logical." I nodded toward Dave.

"Flower Child? You must be kidding."

"I'm serious. I have proof."

On break at the picnic table out back, I was finally able to spill my guts. "So you see, when Dave told me he'd fallen in love with a girl at Woodstock he never saw again, and Grandma Donnie confessed she'd gotten pregnant at Woodstock, it was a no-brainer."

I looked at my Sisters. Skepticism was written all over their collective faces.

Sudsy popped a grape into her mouth. "Brooke, do you have any idea how many people were at Woodstock? Like half a million."

Tamara laughed. "Yeah, and how many of those half-a-million flower children did the dirty deed?"

"And how many of the girls probably got pregnant?" Maria added.

"Okay, you have a point, but there's something really important I forgot to tell you. Her name was Denise."

"And that's your abuelita's name?" Maria looked hopeful.

"No, it's Donna, but they sound the same. Dave said he couldn't remember for sure."

Tamara rolled her eyes. "Can't remember? Damn!"

"And what did Grandma Donnie say?" Maria asked.

"She said his name was Dean."

"Dean? Sorry, but Dean is not Dave," Sudsy reminded me.

"But..."

Tamara crumpled her Fritos bag and tossed it into the trashcan. "I know, but they *sound* the same."

Maria looked solemn. "No wonder my parents won't let me date."

"I wish I'd been at Woodstock," Sudsy said. "Maybe I'll put it in my romance novel. Janis Joplin, Jimi Hendrix—"

"Oh, I forgot to tell you," I said, "guess who I saw at Spring Bayou?"

"Who?" the Sisters asked in three-part harmony.

"Paris Breck."

Sudsy looked at me. "You mean that redhead who got mad when you called her an eponym?"

"Uhhuh."

Maria frowned. "What's an eponym?"

Sudsy waved a hand. "I'll explain later."

"So?" Tamara still wore her bored look.

"She and her daughter Tiffany were in the parking lot looking at stuff they'd bought at the mall, and their Shih Tzu got away."

"And?" Sudsy asked, "did you charge to the rescue?"

"Yeah, I caught the little devil. And as a reward, Tiffany gave me this killer Marilyn clutch."

I grabbed my newest favorite possession from the picnic bench for

33

its Sister debut.

Maria smiled. "I hope Paige Barton and her ladies in waiting noticed it at school. That clutch is not cheap."

"I practically dangled it in their faces."

"Gad!" I'd finally gotten Tamara's attention. "Who'd have thought those stuck up honkies would be that nice."

So that's how it ended. The Sisters loved my Shih Tzu rescue story and my new clutch, and loathed my theory about Dave and Grandma Donnie hooking up at Woodstock. The Sisters were right. I did have a wild imagination.

So okay, I admitted, maybe my recent lack of social interaction, a.k.a restriction, was causing the synapses in my brain to misfire. Maybe I should just concentrate on the Vocabulary Bee and call Chad Roshbaum to see if he wanted to come over and look up definitions. Not very exciting, but with ten days left of solitary confinement, it was better than nothing.

Be careful what you ask for, because two days later who stood on my front porch but Chad Roshbaum—tall and skinny, with wild black curls, radically thick glasses, cornball briefcase, and a large dictionary. I tore down the stairs to open the door, but Benji beat me to him.

"Hello," Chad said.

"Hello," Benji said, looking skeptical. "I don't think we want to buy any encyclopedias."

"I'm not here to—"

I grabbed my brother by his T-shirt. "Benji, please. This is my friend, Chad. Chad, my brother, Benji."

Chad nodded.

"Come on in. We can use the den. It's quiet and has a computer."

"What are you two going to do in there?" Benji's suspicious expression hadn't changed.

"We're going to *study* for the Vocabulary Bee. Now please, go grease the trucks on your skateboard or something."

If you're wondering why Chad was allowed to come over, you have to remember that parents are required by some weird code to do whatever possible to educate their offspring. So, to deny Chad's help when I'd been chosen to represent Coral Cove High in the Vocabulary Bee would have been absolute grounds for a visit from a social worker.

Chad followed me into the den. "You have an incredible home, Brooke. Is it an Addison Mizner?"

"No, but it was built during the twenties. You know, you're the first person who's ever asked me that. Nobody else has ever heard of Mizner."

"Too bad. He was a killer architect. I'd love to visit his houses in Miami."

Sometimes when you don't expect a lot, you're really surprised. I mean, reading words out of the dictionary sounds like the absolute pits, but when Chad started doing charades for clues it was like, pretty funny.

"Brooke, how about this one? I'll give you a clue. *Babbitt.*

"I don't know."

"Okay. Watch this." He held his hands a few inches apart.

"Hands?"

Furious shake of head. He placed his hands together again, this time closer.

"Skinny?"

Negative shake.

"Small?"

Another shake.

"Narrow?

Huge grin and nod.

"Okay, narrow. Second word?"

He touched his head.

"Hair? Head? Brain?"

Chad did a come-on motion.

"Brain, brain. Mind?"

Vigorous nod.

"Narrow mind. Narrow minded!" I screamed.

Chad grabbed me by the waist and twirled me around. His glasses went flying and all I could see was a mass of black curls and a pair of incredible green eyes.

"Sorry," he said, putting me down. "I guess I got, you know, a little carried away. But that was a hard word. By the way, do you see my glasses?"

"No, not really." I stood there, not budging, because for some weird reason I didn't want to look for his glasses or define a new word. I didn't want to do anything except stare into his face.

Magic moments don't last long. That's what makes them magic. And in a minute the old Chad was back—glasses, wild hair and all. But secretly, I felt like an art curator who's just discovered a priceless masterpiece underneath a paint-by-number. And when my new friend and vocabulary coach left and I closed the front door, I knew my feelings toward Chad would never be the same.

Like a prisoner, I marked off the days of restriction on my Far Side calendar. Being a helpless teenager I was used to getting up at the ungodly hour of six, throwing rags on my semi-conscious bod and a hi-pro shake down my gullet, and dragging off to school by the unconscionable time of seven.

What I *wasn't* used to was the Sahara Desert nothingness of after school and weekends. And if it hadn't been for the diversion of my job at Surf's Up and my new infatuation, Chad Roshbaum and his traveling dictionary, I wouldn't have made it.

Fourteen days, or three hundred thirty-six hours, or twenty thousand one-hundred-sixty minutes, and God only knew how many seconds later, I was free. But of course I didn't do the calculating. Chad did it for me.

We sat in the den Saturday night, my last evening of restriction, me watching Chad rummage around in his beat up briefcase. When he was through, he handed me an envelope. Surprised, I opened it to find a handmade card. On the front was a drawing of a prisoner in a striped uniform, with a photo of me from an old yearbook pasted on the head, holding a sign that read *Free at last! Free at last! Thank God Almighty, Brooke is free at last!* Inside was the total time of my restriction in hours, minutes and seconds.

"Oh Chad, I love it!"

"I hope you don't think it's disrespectful," he said. "My family has always been staunch supporters of civil rights. My grandfather was a Freedom Rider in Mississippi in the sixties."

"Oh, no. I think it's wonderful. Thank you."

He snapped his briefcase shut and got to his feet. He looked down at his scuffed Eccos. "I suppose this means we won't be seeing each other anymore."

"What?"

"I mean, now that you're like off restriction and everything, you're probably gonna date Tyler again."

"Oh, no. Tyler and I broke up." I touched his face, turning it toward me. "Chad, I've had a lot of fun these last two weeks, and I'd really miss you if we didn't see each other anymore."

"You would?"

I nodded.

He smiled. "That's cool, Brooke. That's really just so co—"

I stopped him with a kiss. His breath was minty, so I kissed him again.

"Does that mean we're going together?" he asked.

I smiled. Poor Chad. It was like explaining dating to a kindergartner. "No, we're not literally *going together*, but we can go out. Okay?"

"Okay. Okay, okay, okay." He practically skipped down the hall. "I guess I'll like call you tomorrow."

"You do that," I said and closed the front door behind him.

To celebrate my freedom, I met the Surf Shop Sisters at the Parthenon for lunch the next day at the sponge docks. It was a beautiful Saturday—the kind of day Floridians die for. Seventy-two degrees, blue blue skies, Cool Whip clouds, and money in my Dooney and Bourke popsicle purse. Life was good.

Tamara and Sudsy sat at a table on the porch in the back. They clapped when Maria and I showed up.

"They're out!" Sudsy exclaimed, jumping to her feet, causing more than one sunburned touristy-face to swivel in our direction. "Maria! You weren't supposed to be out for another two weeks in exchange for helping him every weekend."

"Don't worry, folks," T announced theatrically. "They're harmless. As for the ankle monitors, they'll be coming off soon."

Maria's face was as red as the checkers on the tablecloth. "Stop, you guys. Sometimes I wonder why I even hang out with you."

Tamara threw a piece of bread in her direction. "Because you can't find anyone else stupid enough to cover for you while you're screwing around, that's why."

"Anthony and I are not screwing around," Maria hissed back. "We went to the Homecoming Dance, that's it."

"Right." Sudsy turned to me. "So how does it feel to be a free woman?"

"I never want to be on restriction again," I said. "Never."

"So what are we eating?" Sudsy asked, changing the subject.

I took off my Panama hat and shook my curls. "I've been dying for dolmades. Dolmades and rice."

"Pricey," T said. "I was thinking more like a gyro."

"Get what you want, T," I told her. "I have money, even after making this month's payment to Simon Legree."

"I almost forgot about your party with daddy's Master Card," Maria said. "How much do you still owe?"

"Two hundred thirty-nine dollars and eighteen cents. He marks it down in a little book. It's really creepy."

Sudsy nodded. "Parents are weird that way."

The waiter lit our Greek cheese and we all yelled *umpa*, then Maria dropped the latest.

"I just wanted you guys to know, Anthony's leaving the Monday after Thanksgiving. He'll be at basic for three months, and then he's going to the Middle East."

"Damned war," Sudsy muttered, and began nervously clicking her mouth.

"Oh, Maria, I'm sorry," I said. "Maybe he'll get to come home after basic."

"No, they're sending him straight over."

I wanted to tell Maria not to worry, but how could I? Only a moron wouldn't worry. They kill people in wars.

Maria pushed away her plate, folding her slender hands in front of her like a teacher about to make an announcement. She took a deep breath. "Anthony wants me to spend the night with him before he leaves."

"You mean like sleep with him?" Tamara yelped. Several heads turned our way.

"Shh!" Maria warned.

A cloud of sanity floated across my brain. "I don't think it's a good idea, Maria. I mean, you could get pregnant."

"Or get AIDS or something," Sudsy added.

"Anthony doesn't have AIDS."

Tamara frowned. "I can't believe you, of all people, is going to have sex!"

"You should talk, T." Sudsy licked a piece of cheese off her finger. "You spent the *entire* night with Jamal. Or have you forgotten that little assignation?"

"Assignation, my ass. You know damn well we didn't do it. And I'm sure Anthony has something that requires a little more testosterone in mind with Maria. Remember, the dude's like nineteen."

"Twenty," Maria said. "He just had a birthday."

Sudsy took another piece of saganaki, then looked at Maria. "So, are you going to do it?"

Maria lowered her eyes. "Well, I know it's a mortal sin, but Anthony's leaving for a whole year..." She looked up, the inevitable tears spilling from behind her thick eyelashes.

"Yeah, he could get killed or something," Tamara said.

I nudged her foot under the table.

"So where is this little Romeo and Juliet scene going to take place?" Sudsy asked.

"The Don Carlos."

"*The* Don Carlos on the beach?" Sudsy screeched.

Maria nodded.

Sudsy fanned her face. "Omigod, just like in my romance novel."

"Damn." It was all Tamara could say.

"He's taking me to the King James Room for dinner first," Maria went on.

I whistled. "My parents ate there on their anniversary, and it cost my dad at least two hundred dollars."

Tamara came out of shock long enough to do one of her shoulder rolls. "Well, I hope Anthony's got a lot of money on his credit card, because he's going to need it."

"He says he wants everything to be perfect. He's incredibly

39

romantic."

Tamara rolled her eyes.

"I'm supposed to meet him at eight, exactly four weeks from tonight. But there's one itsy bitsy, little problem."

We three Sisters looked at each other, waiting for the other high heel to fall. "I don't know how I'm going to get there."

Tamara began tearing her napkin into shreds. "Why doesn't he just pick you up at your house like any other dude?"

"Because my parents hate him, remember? They think he's too old and is a bad influence because he's a dance instructor. My father threatened to have him arrested if he comes within a block of the house."

"Why don't you ride your bike?" Sudsy said.

If she hadn't been so far away, I would have nudged her, too. "You're kidding, of course." One thing you can say about Sudsy, she's practical.

"Well, that way she'll have a way to get home."

Tamara laughed. "Very friggin' romantic."

"Look," I said, "Maria can't ride her bike on U.S. 19 at midnight."

"Do you think it will take that long?" Maria asked.

By now Tamara was destroying another paper napkin. "How the hell do we know, Maria? It depends on what kind of a man he is."

Sudsy assumed her know-it-all look. "Well, sometimes in romance novels the hero and heroine do it for hours."

Tamara snickered. "Bullshit."

The waiter came with the bill. After much adding and dividing, we coughed up the money.

"So, you're saying you want us to drive you to meet him?" Sudsy asked when the waiter left.

Maria didn't answer, but her expression said *yes.*

"And when you're through, take your newly deflowered ass home," Tamara added.

My dolmades began to do a square dance in my stomach. "Maria, I just got off restriction today, and I don't think this is, you know, a very good idea."

"Well, it wouldn't be like *you* guys would be doing anything wrong. I mean, I'm the one going to the hotel room."

I nodded. "True, but we're like, accomplices. Besides, everyone in town knows my convertible."

Tamara sighed. "So, I suppose that means *I'm* driving you to the Don Carlos, since I'm the only Sister, beside Brooke, who has a license."

Maria nodded.

"And, I suppose that means I'll have to bug my dad for his car. You don't want much, do you, girl?"

"Oh, please," Maria pleaded. "I love Anthony so much, and for all I know, I might never see him again." She began to wail. Never mind we were in public.

Tamara threw up her hands. "Well, I guess it's my friggin' patriotic duty. But you two Sisters better be in on this caper too."

Sudsy and I nodded.

"But just this once, Maria," I said. "From then on your love life is absolutely up to you."

"Oh, thank you, thank you," Maria cried, the waterworks coming to an abrupt halt. "You guys are the best."

So it was set. Tamara and Sudsy would pick up Maria four weeks from that night at seven-thirty. Seeing Maria's parents practically had a restraining order against me, they'd swing by Porpoise Drive for me after. Next we'd deposit Maria at the Don Carlos, while we three virgin Sisters hung out until she and Anthony were through doing the deed.

I had a really bad feeling about the whole thing. Driving home I didn't say anything to Maria. But after dropping her off a block from her house, I began some major worrying.

Maria's love life had already gotten me two weeks restriction. And now she'd talked the Sisters into something that could set me up for even more misery. I mean, how much do you owe your friends, anyway? The question played over and over in my head. Just where do you draw the line?

Chapter Six

The weeks hop-scotched by. Cramming for finals, studying with Chad, and working at Surf's Up filled the squares on the sidewalk of my life. And the whole time, hanging out in the back of my mind, were Maria, Anthony, and the Don Carlos. The Sisters and I didn't talk about Maria's big night. I was in my usual denial figuring if I didn't think about it, it would never happen. I mean, the whole idea of Maria going to bed with Anthony was totally unreal, like the steamy plot of one of Sudsy's novels. Girls like us didn't do things like that.

It was the day before Thanksgiving and Tamara and I were at Surf's Up marking stuff down for our After Thanksgiving Sale, when who should trot in but Paris Breck and her sidekick, Tiffany. I did a hair color check (red again), then smiled a professional Surf's Up smirk that Paris returned like a ping-pong ball.

"Hello," she caroled, practically levitating past me toward the rack of Juicy Couture. She had one of those voices that shoots right through you like a laser gun—shrill and fakey. "And how are you today, darling?"

"I'm fine."

"Well, you certainly look tres chic in those white jeans. Makes you look like a Guess model."

I smiled, too overcome to speak, while Tamara gave me a look that could only be translated into *what a bull shitter.* But I ignored her since she was probably just jealous since everyone was always telling her she should be a model.

"By the by, you seem to be a bit low on inventory. There are only two L's in size seven."

"We're getting a ton of new stuff in this weekend after the Thanksgiving Day Sale."

She nodded. "Speaking of Dave, where is that handsome boss of yours?"

As though on cue, Dave appeared from the back office, smiling so hard I thought his face would break.

"I'd recognize that voice anywhere," he answered in an equally bullshit tone.

"That's be-cause I e-nun-ci-ate," Paris said, enunciating each syllable in the most nauseating way imaginable. "This young-er gen-er-a-tion does not take the time to speak prop-er-ly, don't you a-gree?"

"Right on," Dave said, pushing back a strand of straggly hair. "Now, we were totally different. We were interested in intellectual stuff."

"Definitely. Literature, philosophy, the arts."

I looked at Tamara who was biting her bottom lip to stave off hysteria.

"Like music," Dave continued. "At Woodstock some of the songs were friggin' poetry."

Paris struck an OMG pose. "Don't tell me *you* were at Woodstock, too?"

Dave's scrawny chest inflated. "Hell, yeah. Do you think I'd miss a chance to hear Jimi Hendrix?" His arms assumed an air guitar pose. Soon a series of yowls erupted from his mouth. "Dar, dar, dar, dar, dar, dar." It was the Star Spangled Banner mangled beyond belief.

Paris smiled weakly. "Very patriotic."

"Thank you. Hey, if you're into Woodstock, I've got some killer posters in my office if you'd like to see them."

"Why, I'd love to."

Tamara and I watched as the two flower children disappeared around the corner.

"Two guesses what he'd love to show her," Tamara whispered.

I shook my head in the direction of the dressing room where Tiffany was trying on suits.

"Oh hell, she can't hear us."

When Dave and Paris reappeared, they were giggling like a couple of horny freshman emerging from the boiler room at school. Dave's face

43

was flushed, and I could have sworn Paris' lipstick had just flunked the Revlon no-smear test.

God, I hope Paris Breck doesn't turn out to be Dave's Mystery Girl. She was such a phony and Dave, in spite of all of his missing brain cells, was a good guy. Well, I couldn't worry about it. It just seemed kind of funny Paris had been at Woodstock too. But, as Sudsy said, half-a-million people were mucking around in the mud that wild weekend.

Dave was in a great mood the rest of the afternoon. Hey, Paris had called him handsome, and who knows what else had happened in his crammed, messy office? Also, my mom had called and asked him over for Thanksgiving dinner. There was only one problem. Dave had lost his set of keys.

"Have you guys seen my keys?" Dave asked, watching T and me carry in the sign from the sidewalk. "You know, the ones on the Mickey Mouse key chain?"

We shook our heads.

"Did you look in the bathroom?" Tamara asked.

"Or the stockroom?" I added.

"I've looked everywhere. Well, I've got an extra set, but please keep an eye out. I don't want them floating around."

We nodded.

"Alzheimer's," Tamara whispered.

Weather still gorgeous, Tamara and I escaped from Surf's Up. The sun hung over the Gulf of Mexico like a humongous red beach ball. I put down the top of the Green Lady, letting the breeze blow through our hair like we were in a movie.

"Dave's starting to forget everything," Tamara announced from behind her sunglasses.

"Oh, come on. He's too young for that."

"Don't think so. Remember all those drugs he did in the sixties?"

"You don't know that for sure."

"Honey, that's one of the few things I *do* know for sure."

We pulled up in front of Tamara's house. Her dad was in the yard raking leaves. He waved.

"Have a great Thanksgiving, T," I said. I reached over and gave her a hug before she climbed out of the car. "And say hi to your Aunt

Desiree."

"I will. And you say hey to everybody at your house. I'll save you a piece of sweet potato pie."

I drove home thinking about the days ahead—Thanksgiving, Surf's Up's After Thanksgiving Sale, the Vocabulary Bee, and of course, Maria's deflowering. I sighed. I hated to think about Maria losing her virginity.

Not that I wouldn't someday, but I certainly wasn't in any hurry. I had more important stuff to do with my life, like getting through high school. And then going to college and being somebody. I wasn't sure what, but my plans didn't include a night at the Don Carlos any time soon.

With visions of sweet potato pie and turkey legs dancing through my head, I steered the Green Lady toward Porpoise Drive and the old familial nest. But lurking behind every green bean almandine were my suspicions about Dave and Grandma Donnie.

Why did life have to be so complicated? I mean, wouldn't things be a lot simpler if I came right out and asked them if they had done it at Woodstock? But no, I had to kill myself trying to figure out something politically correct.

It wasn't until I'd cruised through our wrought iron gate that my meager supply of brain cells kicked in. I felt the squiggly lines on my forehead unscrunch. A DNA test! They did them all the time on TV shows. Why hadn't I thought of it before?

Tires screeching, I pulled into the garage and jumped out of the car. In the kitchen the smell of cinnamon hit my olfactory senses. My mom was at the counter stirring something in a huge blue mixing bowl.

"Hi, honey. How about peeling some apples for the pie?" she asked. She pointed a wooden spoon in my direction. There was flour on her nose.

"Sorry, but I've got something really important I have to do, like right now."

I ran up the stairs, Erskine hopping behind me. Barely missing his tail, I slammed the door, grabbed my laptop and logged on. Fingers skipping across the keys, I typed until—bingo! There it was! *Home DNA*

& Paternity Testing. Quality Assured.

"Yes!" I yelled. I grabbed a startled Erskine and gave him a squeeze. I could buy a paternity test on the internet! And even cooler, they'd send it to me for the totally reasonable price of $89. Unreal! I exhaled. God bless Bill Gates and the personal computer.

I dove into the web site devouring page after page. Skipping over the really technical stuff, one thing was clear. Whether I chose the blood or spit test, I was going to have a heck of a time getting either one. I imagined my parents, brother, Grandma Donnie, and Dave as we all sat around the living room after Thanksgiving dinner the next day.

Excuse me, Mom, but could you hold still a minute while I jab you in the finger? Or even better, *Please open your mouth while I stick in this Q-tip.*

I needed help. Frantically I grabbed my cell. In a few seconds I'd sent the following text.

Help!! Major crisis. Need U now!!

I guess when parents complain teenagers are always on their cells or computers it's true, because within milliseconds there was an answer from the smartest guy I knew.

R U OK??? Should i come over 2 CU?

Yes. Please Hurry!!!!

I guess you could say most of the time Chad moves at a speed just slightly faster than catatonic, so I was totally surprised when no more than twelve minutes later there was the sound of *Beethoven's Fifth*. I flew down the stairs with my laptop to the front door, but Benji had beaten me to it.

"She's not here," Benji was saying in the most unfriendly tone. "I think she went out on a date with some college guy in a Jaguar."

"I did not, you little Neanderthal," I shrieked, giving Benji a sisterly push. I smiled at Chad and closed the door.

"Wow, you sure made it fast considering you rode your bike."

"Yeah. I drank two YooHoos." He was panting and his pupils looked glazed. "I'll sure be glad when I have a car. My parents promised me one for my birthday."

"Killer." I gave Benji a get-lost look. "Why don't we go out to the gazebo where we can have some privacy?"

I switched on the floodlights to the pitch black backyard. Chad and I made our way over the spongy, damp St. Augustine. I pulled my sweater around me, taking a deep breath of chilly November air.

"So, what's the big crisis?" Chad asked, reaching for my laptop-free hand.

"I'm working on something really personal and I need help in a major way."

We stopped and he put his arms around me.

"Why didn't you call Sudsy?"

"Because I need someone even smarter than she is. Besides, she thinks I'm crazy."

He nodded as though me being crazy was not a new concept. In the gazebo, we plopped down on the glider. Within a couple of minutes, I'd filled him in on the details of my *Who's Your Daddy?* theory.

"Hmm. Surf's Up Dave your grandfather. It's pretty wild. I mean, being related to an old hippie like him."

"I know. That's where the DNA comes in. According to the web site I found, you can use either blood or spit for the test. Here, I'll show you."

I opened my laptop and logged on. In a minute I had the DNA site on the screen.

"Pretty cool stuff," Chad said, swiping the PC from my lap.

"But there's one huge problem." I could feel the squiggly lines on my forehead scrunching up. "I don't know how I'm going to test all three of them without them knowing it."

"You're not."

I sighed.

"But there's another way." He took off his glasses and cleaned them on the end of his T-shirt. I looked into Chad's eyes. Even in the semi-dark they were as green and gorgeous as ever. It was all I could do not to forget the whole DNA thing and just make out with him instead.

"Okay, what?"

He put on his glasses. His long fingers skipped across the keys of the PC. "Here, look at this." And there it was—*Hair DNA Paternity Test*, just like that.

"You're a genius!" I squealed. "Why didn't I think of that?"

Chad adjusted his glasses to hide his Cheshire cat grin. "According to this, all you need is a couple of strands."

"Easy. At least, easier than sticking a bunch of Q-Tips into their mouths."

"Now, Brooke, you'll have to focus. The hairs have to have the *roots* attached."

"So, I'll have to pull them out, not like break them, right."

"Exactly."

"It also says a used Band-Aid or a cigarette butt is okay, but hair's better."

"Got it. Oh, Chad. You are incredibly awesome." Impulsively I leaned over and gave him a really sexy kiss with just a little bit of tongue as a bonus. Surprised, he kissed me back. I was ready to kiss him again when I thought of something.

"There's another problem," I wailed. "I don't have a credit card, and I need the test right away. My dad will never let me use his …."

Chad reached into his jeans. In a second he'd pulled it out. The most beautiful sight I'd ever seen—a shiny silver Visa. I looked at it in awe. *Chadwick W. Roshbaum* in embossed letters.

"Killer! You're the only guy I've ever known with a credit card in his own name."

"My dad thinks it's important to learn how to manage money. I pay the bill every month from my allowance. I have perfect credit."

"You are just so mature, Chad." I thought of Tyler and how I used to pay our way to the movies. It was like comparing Donald Trump to Oliver Twist.

Chad didn't answer. He was too busy filling in the info for the DNA kit. "It should be at your house in three to five days. Don't worry, it will be in a plain brown wrapper."

"I'll pay you back, of course," I promised.

"Sure, whenever."

I smiled. It would have been nice if he'd said just forget about it, but I guess that's not how you get perfect credit. I leaned forward to give him another kiss. It was the least I could do. Things were just getting good when I looked up to see a chubby face with freckles.

"You better go help Mom," Benji said. "She's getting really upset and yelling at everyone."

"It happens every Thanksgiving," I explained to Chad. "She's usually pretty sane."

"It's okay. My mother does the same thing on Rosh Hashana." Chad logged off and snapped the lid. "Well, I guess I better be going. Just do what I told you and everything should work out."

He jumped on his bike and pedaled down the driveway. I watched him as he disappeared through the gate. When I turned, Benji eyed me suspiciously.

"What did he mean by everything working out?"

"None of your business."

"Well, I hope it doesn't mean you're pregnant or anything."

"Oh, don't be such a moron."

I thought of the gentlemanly way Chad had paid for the test with his shiny new Visa and gave him a really good imaginary kiss.

The sound of pans crashing greeted my imbecile brother and me in the kitchen. Our mother stood next to her new state-of-the-art stove, crying on my dad's shoulder.

"It's just that I'm trying so hard..." blubber, blubber... "to make a nice dinner for everyone..." Sniffle, sniffle. "I'm killing myself..." At this point her shoulders shook. "...getting ready for Thanksgiving and no one even caaaares..." Her voice stretched into a wail.

"That's not true, honey." My dad was using his *I-should-have-worked-at-the-UN* voice. "The kids and I appreciate *everything* you do, don't we kids?"

Benji and I nodded on cue.

"Now, why don't you just lie down on the couch, and I'll bring you a nice glass of wine. I'm sure Brooke can take over in the kitchen."

My dad shot me a *you-better-do this-or-I'll-kill-you* look.

"Sure, Mom," I said, with all the bravado I could muster. "What would you like me to do?"

There was a moment of silence while my mom digested this offer.

"Well," she began tentatively, apparently forgetting the D+ I'd gotten in Home Economics last semester. "The pie is in the oven. Take it out when the timer goes off." Sniffle, sniffle. "But I still have to make the rolls."

I smiled confidently. "No problem. We made corn muffins in Home Ec, and they were really easy."

"Yeah, and I'll help," Benji chimed in.

A real smile crept across my father's face. "That would be great."

My mother wiped her eyes on her Kiss-the-Cook apron.

"The dough is rising. When it gets big as a balloon, punch it down. Then make the clover leaves and cover them with a dishtowel so they can rise again. Oh, Bud, it's too much for them," she wailed, looking like she was about ready to have another meltdown.

"No, No. I've watched you make rolls a zillion times, really," I assured her. "It will be fun."

After more of my father's coaxing, they were gone. My brother and I stood at the kitchen sink washing our hands.

"Why can't she just buy rolls at Publix's like everyone?" Benji said.

"Because she's obsessive, Benji. It runs in the family. Now, sit on that stool and read me the recipe so I have it straight."

Things went okay for a while. Benji was a surprisingly model boy right up to when he punched down the dough, *twice,* then defected.

"All right," I told the dough. It looked back at me from its bowl. "I'm sorry Benji was so sadistic when he punched you, but if you'll cooperate, I promise I'll be gentle."

I'd just plopped the last cloverleaf roll into the baking pan when my dad appeared, a fatherly smile pasted on his face.

"Thanks for bailing your mom out, Brooke." It was the first civil thing he'd said to me since the Maria debacle (appropriate vocab word).

"That's okay. It was sort of fun." A total lie, of course, but sometimes you have to tell parents what they want to hear. "Do you think you could do me a favor and put the rolls in the oven when they rise again? I'm really tired."

"Sure. You just run along." And with that, leaned against the oven and burned his hand. I staggered off to bed, a string of my dad's very un-Thanksgiving-like words filling the air.

Exhausted, I flopped on my duvet, quick dialing Sudsy to fill her in on the latest *Who's Your Daddy* melodrama.

"I'm doing the test tomorrow. That way I'll have all the strands ready to mail when the test comes."

"You're going to try to get hair from your mom, grandma *and* Dave?"

"Uh huh."

"And you don't think they're going to notice when you start yanking hair out of their heads?"

"I'll give them all a lot of wine first, then create a diversion."

"Damn." It was all Sudsy could say.

"I can't talk anymore, Suds. I've got to crash."

"Okay, but be sure to call me tomorrow night. All of this *Who's Your Daddy?* stuff will be good in my next romance novel."

"Well, please change the names. I'm in enough trouble already."

"No problem. I have a pseudonym."

I hung up and headed for the bathroom. When all of this was over, *I* might need a pseudonym. Eyes closed, I dragged a tired washcloth across my face, gave my electric toothbrush a minuet around my mouth, and staggered back to bed. But I had a hard time falling asleep. All I could think of was the next day and how I was going to get the hair for the paternity test. Could I pull it off?

Dear God, if you can just help me do this one thing, I promise I will never do anything sneaky again. After helping Maria meet Anthony, of course. Amen.

How do I get into all of these messes? I wondered as I flipped my pillow to the cool side. I thought of how simple my life used to be and sighed. I'll reform, I promised myself. I really will.

Chapter Seven

As far back as I can remember Thanksgiving has been my fourth favorite holiday. But when I woke up the next morning, it had dropped, like the rating of a politician who's done something really stupid.

I reached for Sudsy's vocabulary list on the nightstand. *Thursday, Thanksgiving. Pandemonium—wild uproar.* I shook my head. *For God's sake, Brooke, it's not a horoscope.* All I had to do was stay calm, like a cat burglar lowering herself into the Louvre to steal a Gauguin. Except, I wouldn't have to go through the ceiling, and I was stealing hair.

Okay. DNA subject number one, *my mother.* What a cinch. All I had to do was swipe a few strands of hair from her hairbrush.

Stepping into my parents' room was like entering the Serengeti Plain. White gauze hung from the ceiling, draping dramatically around the four-poster bed. A sexy yellow nightgown lay on a campstool. A faux zebra rug covered the mahogany floor. The only things missing was the bellow of an elephant and a pup tent. I tiptoed across the room into the black granite bathroom. My reflection stared back at me from the mirror.

"Hairbrush, hairbrush, hairbrush," I repeated inanely until I spotted it soaking face down in a washbowl of soapy water.

All right, if she's washing her hairbrush, how about the wastebasket for some hair? From under the sink I pulled out the wastebasket—empty and smelling of disinfectant. Darn it anyway. Why did I have such an obsessively clean mother?

I sauntered down the stairs and sat at the bottom. Benji and the cat were in the foyer chasing a lizard.

"Don't hurt it," I warned.

"I'm not. I'm just going to put him outside."

The chase continued until the terrified creature was corralled into a 7-Eleven cup and dumped out the front door.

"How did the rolls turn out?" I asked.

"Not so great. Dad forgot to take them out of the oven."

More great news. Maybe I should just climb back into bed and go into a coma for Thanksgiving.

"Why do you look so mad?" Benji's face was a foot from mine.

"Benji, will you please back off? My God, do you need glasses or what? I'm just trying to figure something out, that's all."

"Maybe I can help."

Benji? Help? It was a total misnomer (last Monday's vocab word), but what wasn't lately?

"I don't know if I can trust you. You've told every Christmas present since you could talk."

"Yeah, but I've reformed."

I considered my options. "Okay, but this is like crucial."

When I was through whispering my *Who's Your Daddy?* theory, the only sound was the purring of one fat black cat. My little brother's pupils were three-downed Yahoos-wide.

"Damn! You mean Surf Up's Dave is our grandpa?"

"Shh! Not so loud."

"I hope so. Then I can ask him for a surfboard for Christmas."

"Now, listen," I said, ignoring the greed. "At the end of dinner when Mom brings out the apple pie, I want you to create a diversion."

He looked blank.

"Do something to make everyone look at you instead of me. That's when I'll get Dave's hair."

"What about Mom and Grandma Donnie?"

"I'll wait until Donnie is really sloshed, and we'll do Mom now. Come on."

Erskine meowed, and followed Benji and me down the stairs to the kitchen. Our mother sat at the counter drinking tea in her blue silk pajamas, looking fully recovered from her mini-breakdown the night before. She smiled.

"Hi, kids. Beautiful morning, isn't it?"

53

We nodded.

"I just want to thank both of you for doing the rolls last night. I don't know what happened… I mean the crying and everything." She paused. "Maybe I'm just getting old."

"Oh, of course not," I said. "I mean, forty's not old."

"It isn't?" Benji asked.

I gave him a warning scowl. "But, I did actually see a teeny-weeny grey hair yesterday when you were by the pool."

"Grey hair? Oh, no!" From the anguished look on her face you'd thought I said cockroach. "Brooke, you have to find it and pull it out."

For a second I actually felt bad. I mean, how easy was this going to be?

"Okay, I'll see if I can." I ran my hands through her long blonde hair, randomly selecting a hapless hair, and yanked.

"Oww!" she yowled.

"Now, hold still. I see another one." I yanked again. Then again, and again.

"You sure had a lot of grey hairs," Benji said, smiling wickedly. Even Erskine seemed to be laughing.

Excusing myself, I raced to my room. One down and two to go. I sealed the strands of hair into an envelope marked *Mom* and slipped it into my desk drawer. My stomach tightened. Deception and intrigue might seem like fun in the movies, but in real life they made my stomach hurt.

Wistfully I thought of all the Thanksgivings when all I had to worry about was whether I should eat a second piece of pie. But I had to go through with the DNA test. I *had* to find out if Dave was really my grandfather.

In English class Mrs. Ethos is always telling us not to use clichés, but sometimes they come in handy. And whoever the guy was who invented the one about being on pins and needles would have felt right at home at 1502 Porpoise Drive that Thanksgiving.

My alleged grandfather was the first to arrive for dinner. At barely four o'clock the notes of *Beethoven's Fifth* from our doorbell filled the house. I rushed to the front door. There stood Dave looking totally different. I resisted the urge to ask him for his I.D. Instead of jeans and a

T-shirt, he wore slacks and a long sleeved shirt with a collar yet. His long grey hair was neatly slicked back into a ponytail. It even looked like he'd trimmed his ears.

"Happy Thanksgiving, Brooke," he said, handing me a bottle of Burgundy, looking like a kid arriving at a birthday party.

I gave him a hug. "Same to you. Come on in."

"It sure smells great. I can't remember the last time I had a home cooked turkey dinner."

"Everyone's out in the kitchen." I thought of all the Thanksgivings Dave must have spent alone and felt sad. "The other guest should be here any minute."

No sooner had the words popped out than a red SL cruised into the drive and parked in front of our house. The car door opened and, like a model in a Mercedes Benz commercial, Grandma Donnie emerged. Omigod! This was it! An image of Donnie and Dave rushing into each other's arms, smothering each other with kisses and sweet nothings, flashed through my head.

"Wow," Dave exclaimed.

"Wow?" I repeated.

"That's one killer car."

He doesn't even recognize her? I gasped as I watched my grandmother sashay to the front door. *Well, it's been practically forty years, so mellow out.*

"Brooke, my favorite granddaughter," she said when I opened the door. She turned to Dave, a cover-girl smile on her face. "And who may this handsome gentleman be?"

"Grandma Donnie, this is my boss, *Dave*," I said, the name coming out in screaming italics. "And Dave, this is my grandmother, *Donna Dickson*." *The love of your life, you moron.*

Donnie took Dave's hand. "Pleased to meet you. You look awfully familiar. Do you belong to the Yacht Club?"

"No, but you look kinda familiar, too."

Inwardly I tried to picture Dave with the stuffy old guys I'd seen decomposing around the Yacht Club.

Donnie laughed her seductress laugh. "Well, we have all day to figure it out."

Was it possible to fall in love and not even recognize that person forty years later? I wondered, leading the way through the house to the loggia. I guess so. I thought of Tyler. Gad, he was so infatuated with Paige Barton he barely recognized me *now.*

"My God, this looks like something right out of *Lifestyles of the Rich and Famous.*" Dave stood at the edge of the living room, peering out at the porch.

"Well, in our case it's *Lifestyles of the Poor and Infamous,*" my dad said, coming over to pound Dave on the back.

My mother, looking very 1621 Jamestown in brown, floated over like an autumn leaf. "Hello, Dave. So glad you could come. Hi, Mom."

I repeated Dave's words in my head, pretending to see the loggia for the first time, too. Stretching the length of the house, the open-air room overlooked the pool. Stone floor and red-tile-roof-cool, it was indestructible, a limb of the house where Benji and I'd grown up— eating, spilling food and breaking dishes. Fighting over the last piece of dessert, playing *Candyland* at the antique mahogany table, chasing lizards with Erskine around the potted palms. A no-worry, no rules kind of place.

My dad pulled up a wrought iron chair for Donnie, then Dave. "Here, relax. How about a martini?"

Yes! The more booze Dave slugged down, the more out of it he'd be when it came time to yank out his hair.

"I'll have a Bloody Mary, Bud," Grandma Donnie ordered without so much as a *hi.*

My mom turned toward the kitchen. "Now, Brooke, if you'll help me bring out the food from the kitchen. Benji, you can light the candles. Just be careful."

I followed my mother to the kitchen. Maybe I'll work for the CIA when I grow up. I mean, if I can pull off this hair DNA thing, I'll be a shoo-in. I must have had a weird expression on my face.

"Are you okay, honey?" My mom handed me the dish of green beans almandine.

"Sure."

"Sorry again about last night, but..." She lowered her voice. "I'm just starting my period."

I reached for the beans, giving her that special *women-and-our-crosses-to-bear* kind of look.

Most Thanksgivings I eat everything but the tablecloth. But this one it was like I was on the Atkins Diet or something. I mean, how could I eat when I was busy watching and listening to everything Grandma Donnie and Dave did? That and giving meaningful looks to Benji who waited for his signal to create a diversion.

Everyone had been gorging forever, that is, everyone except me who pushed a hapless green bean around on my mother's good china.

"Brooke, are you sure you're feeling all right?" my mother asked.

I nodded. "I'm fine. Just saving room for dessert."

"Why don't you help me bring it out?"

I gulped. *Pie time!* This was it.

Minutes later we reappeared, apple pie, plates, and Haagen-Dazs in tow. Every gluttonous head turned in our direction.

"Now doesn't that look delicious?" my dad bellowed, loosening his belt.

My mother beamed. "Everything turned out beautifully, thanks to Brooke and Benji."

I smiled a guilty smile.

"Now, the first slice is for our guest," Mom announced, plopping a scoop of ice cream on top of a monster slice of pie and placing it in front of my boss.

It's now or never. Positioning my fingers into a plucking mode, I winked at Benji, then moved closer to Dave's mane of hair.

Dave picked up his fork and took a bite of crust. His eyes glazed over. "Oh, God, I think I've died and gone to heaven."

Actually, heaven was a lot closer than Dave realized, for no sooner had the words escaped from his lips than Benji grabbed a napkin and shoved it into a lighted candle. Igniting immediately, it was like someone shot a flame thrower into our Thanksgiving dinner.

My mother screamed. My father swore. And Dave lurched forward to smother the fire, his long ponytail flying into the flame. The moment will be forever frozen in my sixteen-year-old brain—Dave's hair burning, my mother and grandma screaming, my chunky dad dashing to the pool with the fiery napkin, an illuminated Dave at his heels.

By the time Dave climbed out of the pool everything was under control. Fortunately, I'd remembered where the fire extinguisher was. My mom screamed for a while, but who could blame her? Her beautiful Thanksgiving table was covered with poisonous foamy stuff, and one of her guests had been set on fire. Benji was yelping, too, because Grandma Donnie was beating him over the head with the celery stick from her Bloody Mary.

"I always knew there was something wrong with you, Benji," Grandma Donnie ranted.

The only calm one was Dave.

"Call an ambulance," my mom shrieked, watching Dave slosh across the loggia.

"No, no, I'm fine. I didn't even get burned."

My father examined his shoulders. "Are you sure, man?"

Dave held up the end of his charred ponytail. "That's all that burned and I needed a haircut anyway," he laughed. But his eyes weren't laughing.

"Well, everyone kept a cool head," my father said, begging for a compliment for his heroism. "Good job with the extinguisher, Brooke."

"Thanks."

"And as for you, buster." My dad's eyes made the Terminator look like Mother Teresa. "Go to your room."

"It was an accident," Benji mewled, shooting me a dirty look, and tore from the room.

Trembling with fear, my only thought was of escape. "I think I'll get some ointment for Dave's hand."

I ran for the stairs and the safety of the bathroom where I met Benji who was sitting on the toilet seat, looking miserable. I put my arm around his shoulders.

"I'm really sorry, Benji. I didn't mean to get you in trouble, but why did you light the napkin on fire?"

"You told me to create a diversion."

"Yeah, but I didn't say burn the house down."

Benji sniffled.

"It's all right. You were just trying to help."

"Yeah, but now I'm gonna be on restriction and I don't dare ask Dave for a surfboard for Christmas."

"Maybe I can tell Dad that fire's a normal part of an adolescent boy's sexual development."

Benji brightened. "Is it?"

"I don't know, but I'll look it up on the Internet."

"What about the test? We've only got Mom's hair."

"Don't worry. I've got another idea."

Downstairs, Dave had changed into some of my father's clothes that hung on him like a scarecrow. But he didn't seem to mind. Actually, he seemed to be enjoying the attention.

"Well, I'll certainly remember this Thanksgiving," he repeated over and over while my mother and grandma fussed over him.

Box of Band-Aids and ointment in hand, I sat down beside Dave. "Do you mind if I check to see you're okay?"

Nodding, he offered a fiery red hand I accepted with the tenderness of Florence Nightingale.

"Oh, I see a tiny little red mark."

"Naw, that's just an old tattoo."

"No, it's a burn. Let me put some ointment and a bandage on it to be sure."

Grandma Donnie was still shaking. Even her hairspray-helmet hair looked askew. "My goddamned nerves are shattered." Her voice was a mere croak.

"Maybe you'd feel better if you had a cigarette," I suggested.

"God, that sounds good." Donnie's eyes shone.

My mother scowled. "Brooke, your grandmother hasn't smoked for years."

Up for the fight, Grandma Donnie scowled back. "Barbie, I don't see how one miserable cigarette every fifteen years can hurt."

Dave raised his wet head from the pillow. "I think I've got a few smokes in the van."

My grandmother was on her feet before the last word was out of Dave's mouth.

Laura Kennedy

They dashed through the living room like Dave's hair was still on fire. I'm obsessed, I realized as I tore after them through the front door. Like Lady Macbeth I was getting crazier and crazier, and I couldn't stop.

Chapter Eight

Going down for the third time, I frantically struggled to free myself from the dark creature pulling me under the water. My strength all but gone, I gave one last push toward the surface and life.

"Awwk!" Gasping for air, I sputtered to consciousness and morning. "Damn cat!" I yelled pulling Erskine off my face. "Why can't you be happy sleeping at the foot of the bed like any other pet?"

But Erskine was not a normal cat. He had me for an owner and *I* was not normal. I used to be relatively sane, I thought wistfully, as I padded to the bathroom. But now sanity seemed light years ago. Well, hopefully when this *Who's Your Daddy?* and Maria's deflowering thing were over I'd be normal again.

Skipping my morning weigh in, I ambled back to my room. Sitting down at my desk, I removed the three secret envelopes from the top drawer, carefully examining the contents of each. Number 1. *Mom.* Four blonde strands of hair. Number 2. *Dave.* One used Band-Aid. Number 3. *Grandma Donnie.* One lipstick-smeared cigarette butt. Perfect. I had everything I needed for the paternity test.

The day's vocabulary word bounced across my brain. *Apocalypse— a prophetic disclosure.* Couldn't that darn Sudsy pick words that were a little more upbeat?

Half-an-hour or so later, I aimed my convertible for Surf's Up and the chaos of another After Thanksgiving Day Sale. It was a gorgeous morning. A sixty-five degree, clear blue sky with Puff the Magic Dragon clouds kind of morning. So gorgeous I had no choice but to put the top down on the Green Lady.

By the time I pulled up to Surf's Up, I was feeling better. Maybe it was because of the "Bohemian Rhapsody" duet I'd just caterwauled with Queen on the car radio, or because I was wearing oversized Hollywood sunglasses and a Panama hat.

A line of diehard shoppers stood in front of the shop staring at a locked door. Surprisingly, my Sisters were there too. I parked my car in back and ambled to the front.

"Where's Dave?" It was the first time I could remember him being late.

Tamara turned. "I just saw the Tin Can on Wheels turn the corner."

"Maybe Thanksgiving dinner at your house was a little too wild for him," Sudsy added with a laugh.

"Well, actually—" My story was cut short because there, looking like the famous cake left out in the rain, came Dave. Limping to the front door, he unlocked it, standing back for the mini-crowd to surge in.

"Are you all right?" I asked, turning the *Closed* sign to *Open*.

"Just kinda of sore. I must have hit my knee when I jumped into the pool. Couldn't sleep all night."

Sudsy frowned. "You were *swimming* in Brooke's unheated pool in November?"

"Well, not exactly," he answered. "My hair caught on fire, and it seemed like the best way to put it out."

Tamara shook her head. "Sure makes sweet potato pie at our house seem awfully tame."

Maria picked up the end of Dave's ponytail and held it tenderly in her hands, like it was a baby squirrel. "Why don't you let me trim the ends? It will look a lot better."

Obediently, Dave followed Maria back to his office for his free haircut.

Five minutes later I sneaked into the storeroom. Dave was gone and Maria was sweeping singed hair into the trashcan.

"Is everything set for tomorrow night?" I whispered.

She nodded. "Anthony said to be at the Don Carlos by eight because they won't hold our reservation for dinner."

I didn't have to ask Maria if she was nervous. *I'm scared* was written all over her gorgeous face.

The day was crazy. It seemed like every teenager and her or his parent came into Surf's Up. Even Paris Breck and Tiffany showed up. There was no time to gossip with the Sisters. I barely had time to stuff a peanut butter sandwich down my gullet.

I was taking a break at the picnic table, wondering how long it would take for the paternity test to come, when I saw something poking out of the dirt. Actually, the seagull begging for my sandwich saw it first—a bit of blue and red with black ears wedged next to a leg of the table. Dave's keys! I picked them up and brushed the dirt from Mickey Mouse's face. I dashed into the shop where I spotted Dave extolling the virtues of a Blue board to some guy and his dad. Not wanting to blow a big sale, I held the keys triumphantly in the air.

By the end of the day, Dave's grin was as wide as Mickey Mouse's. "The best Thanksgiving Sale ever!" he crowed after the last customer had vamoosed and the front door was locked.

The Sisters and I grinned back.

"And to show how grateful I am, I'm giving you all a Christmas bonus!"

"How much?" Tamara asked avariciously.

Sudsy gave T a disapproving look.

"Wait and see," Dave answered coyly. "And Brooke, thanks for finding my keys. Where were they anyway?"

"In the dirt by the picnic table."

"That's cool. Everything's cool. I am one happy dude." He paused. "Hey, it's raining." Big fat drops of rain bounced off the metal awning. "And the windows are down in my van." He bounded out the back door.

Rain? "Omigod, the top is down on my convertible." I tore out the back door behind him.

Looking back, I wish my story ended there: Dave one happy hippie dude, ecstatic over finding his keys and having a killer retail day; Maria gaga over Anthony; and me preoccupied with the Vocabulary Bee and my *Who's Your Daddy?* theory. But like my English teacher, Mrs. Ethos, always says, a story's not a real story without complications. Maybe that's why things turned out the way they did that weekend.

Chapter Nine

Early morning sunshine tiptoed through the plantation shutters in my bedroom, full of promise and surprise. Saturday and Maria's big day, I remembered, throwing back the duvet. I was happy and sad at the same time. Happy Maria was going to finally have time alone with Anthony before he went to boot camp, but sad too.

Sad that a night that should be nothing but wonderful would be a night of lies and deception. Can love and deception go together? I wondered slipping into my terry robe. Can anything good really come from a bad beginning?

Like I said, to-die-for days seem like they'll never come. But if you don't want a day to hit the old horizon, it pops up before you know it. So when Tamara, Sudsy and Maria picked me up at my house at seven forty-five that cold November night, I was just anxious to get it over with. Kind of like going to the orthodontist to get new braces.

The thump of Los Lonely Boys' "La Bamba" announced the arrival of the Surf Shop Sisters and Tamara's dad's 1987 Chevy. Candy apple red with chrome wheels and a body that practically dragged on the ground, it looked like something out of an old 1970's B-movie.

"Hop in, girlfriend," Sudsy hollered.

I jumped in the back next to Maria. Decked out in a white wool dress that fit her like Saran Wrap, gold hoop earrings and three-inch faux alligator heels, she looked like she'd stepped off the cover of *Vogue*.

"Do I look okay?" she asked, fidgeting with her matching gold bracelet.

"You look beautiful," I answered.

"I just hope it doesn't rain."

Tamara pulled out of the driveway and down Porpoise Drive. I tapped her on the shoulder.

"Tamara, do you think you could turn the radio down? We're trying to look inconspicuous for God's sake."

"You white chicks are so damn uptight."

Defiantly, the music continued to blare. That is until we reached the corner of Kiwi and First Avenue and spotted an aqua and white Coral Cove police cruiser. We drove in relative calm until we reached the Don Carlos. I thought she was pouting, but Tamara must have been thinking instead.

"You know, in that white dress, Maria looks like a virgin about to be sacrificed in a volcano."

Maria whimpered.

"Now, did you bring any protection?" Sudsy asked, ignoring Maria's cry. "You don't want to get pregnant."

Maria nodded. "I bought these."

Tamara pulled into the parking lot and turned on the light. We watched Maria retrieve a shiny packet out of her pseudo-alligator purse.

"Condoms?" I asked.

"Well, they're sure not breath mints," Tamara said.

"Now, be sure not to let him do it until he has one on," Sudsy warned. "Promise?"

Maria bit her lip. "I promise."

"We'll be in the parking lot waiting for you," Sudsy said. "I figure with dinner and everything you'll be gone at least two hours."

"I wish it were summer and we could hang out by the pool," Tamara complained.

"Well, it's November and cold as hell, so we're just going to have to wait for her in the car," I said. That Tamara. Always thinking of herself.

Tamara pulled the Chevy, aka Low Rider, to the front of the Don Carlos. Dramatically pulling her white trench coat around her shoulders, Maria got out. The three of us watched her click up the brick sidewalk where a hunky blonde doorman looked her over like she was a box of Godiva chocolates. But who could blame him?

Maria turned and waved, a brave lamb-to-the-slaughter kind of wave. I tata'd back, silently thanking God it wasn't me.

The Sisters and I sat in a goofy silence. The thought of a two-hour wait looming like detention after school. Tamara and Sudsy must have been thinking the same thing.

"Why don't we go to Movieco?" Tamara suggested. She pulled the car away from the curb. "They've got a new Brad Pitt movie."

Sudsy frowned. "Be serious, we can't leave. Maria might come out early."

"I don't know why soldier boy can't drive her home, for God's sake. It doesn't seem very cool he can steal her virginity and then just kick her out the door."

It was my turn to scowl. "T, Anthony can't drive her home. It's better this way. We don't want Maria to get in trouble again."

Hanging out in an old Chevrolet in the November cold isn't my idea of a great time. Thank God for iPods, headphones, Fritos, and my grey Bear Paw suede boots, because I couldn't have made it without them.

A half hour went by, then another. And then the rain came. Not a quick summer shower, but a cold relentless rain that tried to leak into the old car. I'd just finished playing my new Jonas Brothers album when there was a tap on the window. There stood a drenched Maria. Tear-stained face and hurricane hair.

Tamara rolled down her window a crack. "What are you doing here so soon? You're supposed to be in bed naked rolling around with Anthony. And where's your umbrella?"

"Open the door!" she yowled.

I unlocked the back door and Maria jumped in, shaking drops of water like a wet dog.

"My God, what happened?" Sudsy asked.

"I don't want to talk about it," Maria sobbed. "I just don't want to talk about it."

I put my arm around her. "Are you okay, sweetie?"

She nodded. The only sound was Maria's sobs and the rumble of the Los Lonely Boys on the CD player.

"I just can't believe Anthony wanted me to do such…yucky stuff," she sniffled.

"What kind of yucky stuff?" Sudsy asked, her expression one big question mark.

"Sudsy, please." I brushed back Maria's wet hair from her face. "That's all right. You don't have to tell us."

"All I want to know is if they did it," Tamara said.

The question was enough to send Maria into a new spasm of tears.

It was Sudsy's turn to play sex counselor. "Maria," she began gently, "did you and Anthony make love?"

"Well, if you mean if we actually..." She paused, wiping a tear from her mascara-streaked face.

If Sudsy, Tamara and I had been on a TV soap opera, there would have been a break for a commercial. But being real life, there was only the nervous clicking of Sudsy's tongue against the roof of her mouth.

"Well, I guess I have to say..." Maria hesitated. "No."

"No?" we repeated in unison.

Maria shook her head. "We drank some wine Anthony sneaked into the hotel room. And then we kissed and fooled around. But..."

"Yes?" I said.

"But, when he tried to take off my bra and panties, I panicked. And when I cried, he called me a baby and told me to get the hell out. That he was going to find a real woman."

"What an ass," I said, wishing I could wring his neck.

Tamara started the car, aiming it for the highway and Coral Cove. And if the emotions bouncing around in that 1987 Chevy had been kids, they would have all been on restriction. I mean, as Dave would say, there were real bad vibes in that tin-can-on-wheels—Maria, traumatized; Tamara, mad; Sudsy, surprised; and me just relieved.

And even though it had seemed like there were a lot of reasons for Maria to go to bed with Anthony that night—i.e., they were in love, Anthony going into the military, blah, blah, blah, inside I was doing a big *zis boom bah* because my pre-school pal Maria was still a virgin.

It wasn't even ten, but I was so tired, it felt like I'd been up all night. All I wanted was to put on my flannel pajamas and sleep forever. The thought of my feather duvet covered bed seemed like Shangri La. Being persona non grata at Maria's house, I was dropped off first. The lights from the driveway illuminated the house. I punched in the code and we buzzed through the wrought iron gate.

"Thanks for everything," Maria whispered. I gathered my Maria

67

vigil supplies and opened the door.

"No problem," I answered. "You'd do the same for me." The thought played a nasty game of *What If* while I traipsed through the front door. Would Maria spend two hours camped out in a freezing car in the rain with Sudsy and Tamara while I played house with Chad Roshbaum? Somehow I didn't think so. Besides, Chad would never meet me in a hotel room at the Don Carlos. Tyler, yes, because he was still crazy about me, even if he didn't know it. But being the son of a rabbi, Chad had to practically walk on water or whatever the equivalent is when you're Jewish.

Which reminded me of the Vocabulary Bee competition. Now that Maria's virginity was no longer a hot topic on my frontal lobe, I had something new to worry about. Because a week from tonight I'd be sitting on the stage in Tampa defining words like my life depended on it.

Chapter Ten

I poked my pug nose out from my feather duvet. Recharged and full of goodwill, I skipped to the window to fling open the shutters to see how the world looked at almost noon. Spanish moss dangling from one-hundred-year-old oaks, egrets on the lawn, and an aqua and white Coral Cove police cruiser parked in the red brick drive. Police cruiser? I rubbed the sleep from my eyes. Had my dad watered the grass on the wrong day again?

Worry followed me and my bunny slippers down the stairs. I peeked into the living room. Side-by-side on the couch, wearing matching terrified expressions, perched my parents. Across from them, in an antique planter's chair, sat a man. Thirty-something, Greek and hot, he wore grey slacks, a black shirt and a dark expression.

"Oh, Brooke," my mother said when she saw me. Her voice aimed for a there's-nothing-to-worry-about tone, but failed the audition. "We were waiting for you to wake up."

"Sit down," my father ordered. "This is Detective Stavrakidis from the Coral Cove Police Department. He wants to ask you some questions."

Omigod! Someone had seen Maria and Anthony sneak into the hotel room at the Don Carlos and now we were all in trouble. I tried to look innocent.

I looked at Detective Stavrakidis who'd plastered a pretend smile on his gorgeous mug. "I'd like to talk to you a few minutes, Brooke. Okay?"

Like I had a choice. "About what?" I looked down at the Oriental rug.

"About something that happened last night. Could you tell me where you were? Your parents say you weren't home."

Where was I? How could I say I was playing madam for Maria? "Just riding around with the Sisters."

"The Sisters?"

"My friends Sudsy, Tamara, and Maria. They work with me at Surf's Up on the sponge docks."

"Riding around where?"

"Just around."

Detective Stavrakidis looked skeptical. "This morning a burglary report was made by the owner of Surf's Up. He discovered a large shipment of merchandise missing when he opened."

"The store was robbed?"

My mind did a couple of Ferris wheel turns. Why was he telling me all this?

"There was no sign of a forced entry," he went on. "And according to Mr. Brennan, no one else but him has a key."

"Uh-huh. Dave never gives a key to anyone."

"You're saying you know nothing about the robbery?"

So the cops thought I had something to do with it? Inside I was jumping off that imaginary Ferris wheel; outside I tried for cool and calm. "Why would I?"

"Mr. Brennan said he lost a set of keys last week. He also said you were the one who found them."

A run for your life sign flashed through my brain. "Yeah, I found them in the dirt in back of the store."

"Are you sure you didn't make a duplicate set for yourself?"

My stomach fell down to my bunny slippers. "You mean you think that *I* stole that stuff?" I gave my parents a desperate look.

My mother jumped in. "Brooke has never stolen anything in her life."

"Then, why did I find *this* stuffed in the backseat of her vehicle?" With a flourish he pulled something out from under the cushion of the chair like a rabbit out of a hat. But it wasn't a rabbit. It was a brand new Juicy Couture swimsuit, tags and all. The same white two-piece Juicy Couture I'd told everyone I'd die for. An I-just-committed-treason look crossed my mom's face.

"We gave Detective Stavrakidis permission to search your car."

Coral Cove's finest looked like he'd just won an Oscar at the Academy Awards. I felt like I was going to faint. How had that bikini gotten in the back seat of the Green Lady?

"Believe me, I don't know how it got there."

"What about the other girls who work at the shop?" My mother's voice sounded more confident than she looked. "Maybe they know something."

"We've questioned each of them at their homes this morning, and their alibis are all pretty vague. Unfortunately for Brooke, she's the only who has any of the merchandise."

My father stood up. I was grateful for every ounce of his two hundred-forty-pound bod. "Okay, that's it. Brooke's not saying another word without a lawyer."

Interview over, Detective Handsome got up and pushed a business card into my father's hand. "If you have any questions, please call me."

"Are you pressing charges?" My mother's lip quivered.

"Not at this point. However, I am taking this swimsuit with me as evidence."

He jammed a card in her hand, too. The front door slammed and I collapsed on the couch. "I didn't do anything," I sobbed. "I swear to God, I didn't steal that suit."

"We need a lawyer," my mother said, picking up her cell. "I'm calling Rupert Wilkins."

My father came over and hugged me. "I believe you, Brooke. You do a lot of crazy things, but you're not a thief."

My teeth chattered. *Please, God, make Mr. Wilkins help me.* He should be able to help me get out of something I didn't do. Shouldn't he?

We drove to meet Mr. Wilkins at his office in silence. They were already putting up Christmas lights on Coral Boulevard, a reminder that life goes on, even when your own life is in the toilet.

Rupert Wilkins's office was in the Ponce de Leon, a really old brick building downtown. A brass plaque on the outside said 1940. Every time I went there it seemed like my life turned into an old black and white movie. And today black really fit my mood.

Mr. Wilkins met us at the front door.

"I really appreciate you meeting us on Sunday," my mom began, "but as I told you on the phone, it's an emergency."

"That's perfectly all right, Barbara. Emergencies have their own time schedule."

He turned and we followed him through the marble foyer.

If you ever saw the movie *To Kill a Mockingbird* with Gregory Peck, you know what Rupert Wilkins looks like—tall, thin and kind of old, with a deep voice, and suspenders that peek out from under his grey suit jacket. The only major difference between the movie star and my new lawyer was that Gregory Peck was white and dead, and Rupert Wilkins is African-American and very much alive.

Inside his office was 1940s too. It even smelled old. Leather bound books filled floor-to-ceiling bookcases. Wooden filing cabinets crammed with yellow files of Coral Cove secrets lined the walls like sentries. Four green leather armchairs circled a large mahogany desk and the man who sat behind it. The man who could save my life.

Terrified, I hunkered down in one of the chairs, the only noise being the chattering of my teeth and the squeak of old leather when I reached for my mother's hand.

Mr. Wilkins looked at me like he was looking into my soul. "Well, Brooke, I'm sorry our first meeting has to be under such inauspicious circumstances."

"Me too," I mewed.

"Your mother gave me an outline of what has transpired." He paused. "But before I agree to accept your case, I'd like to hear what happened from you."

I nodded.

"I advise complete disclosure, even if means involving your friends. If not, I will be of little service."

Involving my friends? How did he know I'd be involving my friends? I gulped. It was obvious the *riding around in the car* explanation wasn't going to fly. For an old guy, Mr. Wilkins was pretty smart. I took a big breath of musty air.

"Well, I have this friend and you know, she has this friend, a g—" The *g* stuck in my throat.

72

"Would you like a glass of water?" Mr. Wilkins asked.

I nodded.

My mother dashed off for a bottle of Zephyrhills, while I studied the red Oriental rug. There was no good way to do this. A couple of minutes, a slug of water, and two more garbled attempts later, I was sort of okay. And once I began to spill my guts, it wasn't too hard.

"And that's everything?" Mr. Wilkins asked when I was done, his eyebrows arching like twin caterpillars.

"Yes."

"And the only reason you didn't tell the police what *really* happened is because you were protecting Maria?"

"Yes."

"Oh, Brooke." The two sad words from my mom fell like wounded sparrows.

There was silence except for the sound of Mr. Wilkins snapping his suspenders. "All right, Brooke, I believe you. The fruit never falls far from the tree, so therefore I must."

I breathed for the first time that day.

"But..." he went on, "just because I believe you, doesn't mean the police will. I'm sure this Maria friend of yours won't want to tell the truth. I know Anthony, and he's quite a bit older than you girls, is he not?"

"He just turned twenty and Maria's still sixteen."

"In this state, sex between a minor and an adult constitutes statutory rape, even if it's consensual."

"But they didn't really do it."

"So you said. Well, for now I need to concentrate on proving your innocence." "Do you think you can?" my mom asked.

"I'll do my utmost, Barbara, however, there are still the issues of the mysterious appearance of the bathing suit and Brooke finding the keys."

I squirmed in my chair. "The keys were just a coincidence. Dave must have dropped them in the dirt. And the swimsuit... I don't know how it got in my car."

"Indeed." Mr. Wilkins had gone from suspender snapping to bouncing the eraser end of his pencil on his desk. "Well, we'll just have to wait to see how this unfolds. I'll talk to the detective on the case and see what I can work out. Meanwhile, Brooke, mind your p's and q's. Maybe we'll get lucky and the police will find the real thieves."

"Oh, Mr. Wilkins. Thank you so much." My mother was practically genuflecting.

By the time I holed up in the gazebo in our backyard, I had six text messages and five e-mails. Sudsy sounded the most hysterical so I called her first, then hooked up with Tamara on a two-way. Maria didn't answer. I recapped the day, ending with Rupert Wilkins' last words.

"He told me to mind my p's and q's."

"It means mind your pints and quarts," Sudsy explained. "That's what the English bar maids used to tell the guys in the pubs when they were getting ripped."

"Whatever." It was annoying when Sudsy played *Trivial Pursuit* with my life. "So, what happened when the cops came to your house?"

"Well, my parents were like hysterical. And my Aunt Sophia, who just happened to drop by after church, kept saying, 'Where have we gone wrong?' over and over. But it was in Greek, so it sounded worse."

"Did they charge you with anything?"

"No, but Detective Stavrakidis kept insinuating the four of us were in on the theft. He searched my car too, but of course he didn't find anything."

"How the hell did that suit turn up in the Green Lady?" Tamara asked.

"I don't know, T. Honest to God."

"I believe you. You're the last person in the universe who'd lift anything. Besides, why would you steal when you're rich?"

Apparently, Tamara had never heard of kleptomania.

"What's going on with Maria?" I asked.

"Who knows? I guess the Hispanic Gestapo confiscated her cell." Sudsy sounded furious.

"Well, I had an e-mail from her. Basically, it just said 'Boo. Help, help! Love M.'"

"She always wants frigging help," T said. "I bet you lunch she lied through her teeth."

"Well, I sure don't think she admitted she was in a hotel room with a

74

twenty-year-old guy." As usual Sudsy was all logic.

There was the sound of a male voice. It was T's dad, and he didn't sound too happy.

"Hey, my dad's yelling for me to help with dinner, so I better go."

"Okay, but both of you have to promise you won't say a word about this tomorrow at school. I'll kill myself if anyone finds out."

"Are you kidding?" Tamara sounded incredulous. "This is the last shit I want to get around."

"Me either," Sudsy added.

The last time I cried myself to sleep I was twelve and just got braces. But I would have taken a hundred trips to the orthodontist if I could have taken back last night. My new bamboo pillowcase was wet with tears.

How had my life gotten so screwed up? Maria and Anthony, that's how, the little voice in my head answered. Maria was the one who laid a guilt trip on me so I'd come up with the sleepover so she could go to Homecoming. And then as soon as I got through with two weeks' restriction, she'd talked Sudsy, T, and me into the roles of ladies in waiting while she played hide and seek with her virginity.

I should have told Detective Stavrakidis the truth, but hindsight is always twenty-forty. But I had Rupert Wilkins now. Maybe he could get me out of this mess. That is, if the Coral Cove police didn't decide to charge me with grand theft for the rest of Dave's stolen stuff.

Dave. I hadn't even thought of how bummed he must feel. Like, totally violated. Especially, since he'd come to our house for Thanksgiving dinner and everything. Now he probably hated me even more.

I remembered the three envelopes in my desk drawer. The envelopes with the stuff to prove Dave was my grandpa. What did it matter now? I mean, even if we were related, I doubted he'd want to be a grandfather to a juvenile delinquent.

But I didn't do it! Somehow being blamed almost made me feel like I *had* robbed Surf's Up. Now, don't freak out, Brooke, I told myself. All you have to do is find the person who did it.

But who? I didn't hang around with thieves. I didn't even know anyone remotely suspicious. Obviously it wasn't one of the Sisters. I thought of all my second tier friends. Hmm. Even though I loathed Paige Barton, I knew she didn't have the guts to break and enter. Maybe I should check out the sponge docks to see if I could spot anyone suspicious. In the movies it always looked so easy to spot the bad guy. Attaché cases, fake mustaches and wigs. Wigs! Paris Breck? Hadn't she been wearing a blonde wig the day I'd met her at Spring Bayou and her dog had run away? And hadn't she and Tiffany been fooling around with stuff in the trunk of her pink Caddy?

Chapter Eleven

I would have given anything not to go to school on Monday—my new Andy Warhol Marilyn Monroe purse, my collection of baseball caps, even Erskine. Well, maybe not my cat, but you get the idea. I considered pulling a sick act, but knew it wasn't a good idea. My parents were frosted enough at me already.

So with a lamb-to-the-old-slaughter kind of heart, I pointed the Green Lady in the direction of Coral Cove High. The Surf Shop Sisters met me outside the main door. They were a glum little group.

Maria was actually glum and sweet, a complete oxymoron, complimenting me on my Marilyn purse and Tamara on her hair. She even told Sudsy she looked slimmer. Actually, I think Maria would have gotten down on her and knees and polished my Eccos if I'd asked. Because even though Maria isn't exactly a genius, she's smart enough to know all her BFFs were ready to kill her.

"I'm really, really sorry about Saturday night," she began as we departed en masse (killer vocab word) toward my homeroom.

"What-ever," I answered.

"But how did I know the store was going to be robbed the same night I met Anthony at the Don Carlos?"

"Shut up, Maria," Tamara hissed, looking around to see if anyone had heard her. "You are so incredibly uncool."

Maria assumed a hurt expression, but for once I didn't care.

"You didn't know, Maria," Sudsy said. Maybe Sudsy could get a job with the UN after college.

Tamara wasn't in the mood for diplomacy. "Yeah, well maybe I wouldn't have sounded so damn guilty when that detective questioned me if I could have told him where we *really* were."

Tamara was right. If Maria hadn't been busy playing house with Anthony, we wouldn't have come off so lame. Anger exploded inside me like kernels of Orville Redenbacher.

"You know, Maria, it really makes me mad that you still have a job at Surf's Up and I don't," I said, glaring.

Maria blushed. The only sounds were Sudsy's tongue clicking against the roof of her mouth and the bell ringing.

"I'm sorry. I really am."

Tamara turned her head for a parting shot. "Well, are you sorry Dave gave you all of Brooke's hours instead of Sudsy or me? I wonder why that was? Probably because you're such an angel."

I meandered to my homeroom, plunking down at my desk for ten minutes of announcements over the intercom.

"Good morning, Coral Cove students." It was Mr. Chambers, our principal. "Coral Cove has a busy week ahead, beginning with a home game against our biggest basketball rival, Fort Meyers High, tomorrow night."

Mr. Chambers couldn't have been more ignored if he'd been talking to those huge terra cotta soldiers they dug up in China. I scrutinized my listless classmates. Did any of them know I'd been questioned by the cops? They didn't act like it, because if they did, there would have been a lot of whispers and weird looks. Especially from head Gossip Girl, former friend and boyfriend stealer, Paige Barton, who sat in front of the room.

By afternoon I was starting to relax. Maybe no one at school would ever find out and I could keep my life of crime to myself. It wasn't until the end of fifth period the other high heel dropped. Mr. Wiggins, my world history teacher, brushed by with a note he dropped on my desk like an owl in *Harry Potter*.

Brooke, Please go to Mrs. Ethos' office immediately. C. Chambers

I mean, couldn't he have just *said* it instead of creating all the melodrama and making every student in the class wonder what was going down? But I guess the world thrives on that kind of stuff. That's why housewives watch soap operas. It was about the Vocabulary Bee, of course. Seeing as it was this coming Saturday night and everything, she was probably going to give me a little pep talk.

Chad was just leaving Mrs. Ethos' classroom when I crept in. He had a funny look on his face.

"Hi," I said. "I'll meet you at the bike rack when I'm through, okay?"

He nodded, but didn't smile. Probably bummed we didn't go to the movies Saturday night.

There was no smile from Mrs. Ethos, either. "Hello, Brooke," she said. "Sorry to steal you from history class, but I needed to catch you before you left. Sit down."

For some reason, when an adult tells me to sit down, I always want to run out the door, screaming like I'm one of Henry VIII's wives.

"I'm afraid I have some disturbing news." She paused.

I grabbed my Marilyn purse, ready to make my getaway.

"I've received a message from Mr. Chambers that you were..." She paused for the right word. I guess she had trouble with her vocabulary sometimes too. "Were involved in an unfortunate incident over the weekend."

I gulped.

"Therefore, I'm afraid you will be unable to represent Coral Cove in the Vocabulary Bee."

It felt like an icicle had been stabbed through my heart.

"But, Mrs. Ethos, I didn't do anything wrong. I swear I didn't steal that swimsuit. I have a good lawyer and, well, like, he believes I'm innocent. And I am."

I was about to cry and Mrs. Ethos looked like she was too. "Brooke, I believe you also, but I'm afraid I have no authority over the situation. Mr. Chambers insists everyone representing our school must have an unblemished reputation. I'm sure you understand."

"No, I don't understand. Because I didn't do it!" I slammed my hand down on Mrs. Ethos' desk knocking her glass seagull paperweight to the floor. "It isn't fair! It just isn't fair!"

I turned and ran from the room. So much for being innocent until proven guilty. I jammed on my sunglasses. *Unblemished reputation.* The words chased me as I ran down the hall.

I swung my car out of the parking lot, forcing myself to slow down for the speed bumps. So that's why Chad had looked so weird. Mrs. Ethos had told him. What a narc, but I guess she had to. He would have wondered where I was when I didn't show up at the Vocab Bee Saturday night.

I scratched *meet Chad at the bike rack* from my mental list. It was the last thing I wanted to do. I mean, like, what could I tell him?

A comforting chocolate malt greeted me at the Tastee Freeze. Maybe the chocolate would shoot a few endorphins through my demoralized bod. Besides, I needed a place to sit quietly to think about how to prove Paris Breck robbed Surf's Up.

I tore a piece of lined paper from my notebook. At the top, in neat letters, I printed *Brooke's Plan.* Gad, all of the stress was making me think of myself in the third person, like Donald Trump. Pretty soon I'd be calling myself *The Brooke.*

Number 1. Habitat. Paris Breck probably was kind of rich. So that meant she didn't live in a cute little wooden Cracker house like Tamara or in a mansion on the Gulf of Mexico.

And even though she was old, she was kind of cool, like my Grandma Donnie. That meant she wouldn't wreck her nails cutting grass or washing windows. She'd live in a place where they did it for her. That was it. Ms. Eponym lived in a condo. I grabbed my notebook and my malt and ran to the Green Lady.

I drove down Gulf View Drive, turning in at the first high rise. Egret Place. Waterfront, upscale. Definitely Paris Breck's image. Ready to drive through the wrought iron gate, I stopped. Damn. I'd forgotten they had guards at these places. A really old guy who looked like he should have been at home watching reruns of the *Price is Right* hopped out of the guardhouse.

"Who ya here to visit?" he growled. Why is it that some people think they don't have to be polite to kids?

"Paris Breck."

He scanned a list on a clipboard. "We don't have anybody by that name. Sure ya got the right complex?"

No, I am not sure I have the right complex. Actually, the only thing I am sure of is I just hogged down a thousand calories of chocolate malted for the second day in a row.

It was a repeat performance at the next five places. It was with a blackguard's (cool new word) heart, I pulled up to Point Omega, the digs of Grandma Donnie.

The guard recognized me and smiled. "Donna Dickson, right?" He looked pleased with himself for remembering.

"Right."

But I didn't want to see Donna Dickson. Not when Donnie probably knew about the stuff that had gone down this weekend.

I drove around looking for Paris' pink Caddy. The names of the streets were maddeningly redundant. Point Omega Drive, Point Omega East, Point Omega West, Point Omega Terrace. My God, what was wrong with these people?

I drove past Grandma Donnie's building, hoping she wouldn't spot me. Maybe she was out selling real estate. On to the next building and the discovery some of the condos had garages. How was I going to find Paris' car if it was in a garage?

I pulled into a visitor parking space and turned off the engine. Okay, since only Superman had X-ray vision, I'd have to look around. But I needed a disguise. Panama hat, windbreaker, oversized Hollywood sunglasses. Ready.

Halfway around the building, I spotted it. Omigod! Like a huge glob of pink bubble gum, there it sat. Paris Breck's Caddy!

Casually meandering to the driver's side, I squinted through the window, hoping to see something incriminating. But there was nothing except a bottle of 50 SPF sunscreen and a white denim jacket.

Well, what did you expect, Brooke? Did you think she'd have the stolen stuff lying around in the backseat?

Maybe she'd hid it in the trunk. Just for the fun of it, I hit the trunk *Open* button on my key chain, but nothing. I was figuring out my next strategy when I heard a screech and looked up.

"What the hell are you doing?" It was Miss Eponym in person. *I'm-going-to-kick your-ass* was written all over her too-much-make-up face.

"Oh, I'm selling Girl Scout cookies," I said, jumping about a foot in the air.

"Well, I don't see any damn cookies and I don't live in my car."

"I know," I stammered. "I was just admiring your Cadillac. It's so cool."

She scowled, obviously not buying either my Girl Scout or auto-buff story. She squinted at me behind my disguise. "Haven't I seen you somewhere?"

"Maybe at the Tastee Freeze. I work there."

"Well, Miss Tastee Freeze, get the hell away from my car or I'll call the c—"

I interrupted her mid-word. "I'm leaving right now. Actually, I'm late for my scout meeting."

In the newspaper they're always yapping about how teenagers are out of shape. I just wish they could have seen how fast I ran to the Green Lady. I mean, like if I was in a contest, I probably would have won a gold medal. Hmm, maybe I should go out for track in the spring. Then I remembered—they probably wouldn't want a girl with a *blemished reputation.*

I drove home, trying to cheer myself up. I'd figured out where Paris Breck lived, hadn't I? But it didn't prove anything. Maybe she *hadn't* robbed Surf's Up. Which left me permanently persona non grata, a vocab word I'd never thought I'd be. I heard a ding and looked at my cell. A text from Chad.

By December it was beginning to look a lot like Christmas, especially around Spring Bayou. Lights strung in the palm trees, red ribbon on the docks, and a humungous wreath on the clubhouse door. Too bad I felt like Scrooge. As Dave would say, everything was a bummer.

It was like seventy degrees. I parked and put the top down on the Green Lady, turning my face to the sun for a few rays. Closing my eyes, I tried to calm down by singing 'HU', a word Sudsy told me would mellow me out. I was HU-ing away when I heard a car pull up. I opened my eyes to see a really cool silver Sebring convertible. Behind the wheel sat a hot looking guy wearing designer sunglasses, Chad Roshbaum. He gave me a weak wave.

"Omigod, Chad, is it yours?"

"Yeah. It's only five years old." But instead of sounding happy, his voice was flat and weird.

I got out of my car and hopped over to the driver's side of the Sebring, taking off my shades to get a better look.

"It's beautiful. I thought your parents weren't going to buy you a car until your birthday?"

"It was my birthday last Wednesday, Brooke. Obviously you forgot."

Damn. I looked away in embarrassment. Now I knew what I heard in Chad's voice was hurt. "I'm sorry," I apologized, "but I don't think you even told me."

"Yes, I did. But then, you've been busy."

Only eight words, but it was like he'd written a book. Like a gazelle, Chad threw a leg over the side of his convertible and climbed out.

"I'll make it up to you," I promised. "I'll make you a cake or something."

"Forget it. It's too late."

For once, I had nothing to say. I put my sunglasses back on to hide the tears that were puddling in my eyes. Without a word he took off through the park and sat down on a bench. I followed, like a squirrel hoping for a peanut.

"Brooke, I have to talk to you," Chad said after I plunked down beside him.

Oh boy, here it comes. He's majorly frosted over this birthday thing.

"About what?" The moment had a real déjà vu kind of feeling, like the last time I'd talked to Tyler.

Chad took off his aviator glasses. I looked into his eyes. They were as hard and cold as emeralds.

"I know what happened," he said.

"You do?"

"At first I only thought you were disqualified from the Vocabulary Bee. Then Sudsy told me the rest."

That darned Sudsy. She'd tell anything for attention.

"Did she tell you I'm *innocent*? That we're innocent? Did she tell you the part about Maria and Anthony?"

"She told me the whole thing."

"And?"

"And, even though I believe you didn't steal anything, I just…"

"Just what?"

"Listen, Brooke, I really like you. But having you as a girlfriend is like riding Space Mountain at Disney World every day."

There was a moment of silence. I started to HU again to myself.

"It's not just this Surf's Up thing. My dad opened my Visa bill yesterday and saw the charge for the DNA test."

"Omigod!"

"So, he thought I'd knocked somebody up."

"Did you tell him you bought it for me because I don't have a credit card?"

"Yeah, and then he thought I'd got *you* pregnant."

"You're kidding!"

"He even threatened to call your parents."

A scenario of a bushy bearded Rabbi Roshbaum sitting in our living room with my parents flashed through what was left of my mind.

"Don't worry. I convinced him the test was for your grandmother. All he said was, 'Isn't she a little old?'"

I laughed for the first time that day. But Chad wasn't laughing. He looked at the ground, shuffling his Crocs in the dirt.

"There's something else. My dad said I have to break up with you."

"Break up with me?" Someone was breaking up with me again? I felt like I'd been smacked in the face with a wet yarmulke (vocab word Chad taught me).

"He says you're a bad influence. I'm sorry, Brooke, but you know, him being a rabbi and everything, we have our reputation to think of."

"But I thought you, like, loved me."

"I do, but…"

He reached for my hand. I knocked it away, just like they'd taught me in karate. I was like Mount Vesuvius erupting.

"You know, when you first started helping me with my vocabulary, I thought you were a geek like everybody said."

Chad winced, like I'd thrown a rock.

"But I learned to like you, because I found out who the *real* Chad Roshbaum was. And I thought you knew who the *real* Brooke Bentley was. But now, when it's time to stand by me, you chicken out. You're a major wimp, Chad. A wimp who doesn't have the balls to think for himself."

I turned and sprinted for the Green Lady, the sound of Chad calling my name chasing me.

Everybody hated me! Okay, my parents still loved me, but that was their job. But what about Chad? Isn't your boyfriend supposed to stand by you too? *A bad influence.* Maybe I *was* a horrible person. It didn't matter I was only trying to help my friend. But look where it had gotten me? I felt like a martyr, like Joan of Arc.

I drove on autopilot until I came to Coral Boulevard where I made an abrupt right, slammed on my brakes and parked. Nick's Barber Shop. Men's and Women's Regular Hair Cuts $10.

I shot through the door. The shop was empty except for an old Greek guy in a chair reading a ratty *Swimsuit Edition* of *Sports Illustrated.* I dragged over to a barber's chair and sat down.

"I want a haircut." There were tears in my voice.

He put down the magazine. "Are you sure? I'm not a fancy salon."

"I don't care."

He held up a strand of my hair. "Just a trim?"

I shook my head. "I want it all off. Like a guy."

"A man's haircut? But honey, you got such a beautiful head of hair."

"Just cut it."

He shrugged. "Okay, the customer's always right."

I closed my eyes. It was quiet except for the snip, snip of the scissors. Each snip like a cut into my soul. No one liked me. No one believed me. It didn't matter I was innocent. Like I'd told Mrs. Ethos, it wasn't fair. Life wasn't fair. But I'd get even. I'd find out who did this to me if it took the rest of my life.

Chapter Twelve

The owner of Beautiful You Wig Shoppe was just flipping the *Open* sign to *Closed* when I pulled up. She stopped mid-flip when she saw me standing there in my Panama and sunglasses.

"We're closed," she mouthed through the glass.

"But I have something for you."

Annoyed, she unlocked the door and opened it a crack. "Sorry, but we close at five-thirty, so maybe you can—"

"But I just want to give you this."

She sighed, then opened the door all the way. I handed her a plastic Gap bag. She peeked in. "Yours?" she asked, pulling out what once had been my long blonde hair.

I nodded.

She took off my Panama hat and ran her fingers through my blonde stubble.

"I just wanted to do something good for a change," I said. "Maybe you can make a wig for some teenage girl like me, who's sick."

"Oh, honey, what a beautiful, selfless thing to do." Tears welled up in her eyes.

I started to sniffle too. I was so mad at myself. I never cry in front of people, but there I was, totally losing it.

She grabbed a Kleenex from her pocket and handed it to me. I wiped my nose and she put the Panama back on my head. "Thank you," she said. "This hair will mean a lot to someone. I'll pay you of course."

I shook my head. "No, it's a gift." I turned and walked away.

I got in the Green Lady and headed home, stopping at the first light to take off my Panama and look at myself in the rearview mirror. Mine

86

was a face I barely recognized. I felt like the woman in the nursery rhyme who said, *"If my little dog does not know me, it is not I."* But it was me all right; a really mad me.

Within minutes I was in front of my house on Porpoise Drive, punching the buttons to open the wrought iron gates. I cruised through the driveway and into the triple garage. In the kitchen, my mother hovered over a huge pot of boiling water.

"Hi, honey. We're having spaghetti. The pasta will be done in a couple of minutes, so don't wander off."

"I'm really not hungry. Think I have a touch of the flu."

"Would you like some chicken soup instead?"

"No thanks."

I stumbled through the kitchen, heading for the safety of my room. Obviously my parents were bound to find out about my hair, but I wanted to put it off as long as possible. I was half way up the stairs when I heard a psst. There in the entry was my brother holding a small package in a plain brown wrapper.

"Don't bother me, Benji. I'm in a hellacious mood."

"Me, too. But I got to tell you something. It came."

"What came?"

"The test, stupid."

Omigod. I'd forgotten all about Dave and my *Who's Your Daddy?* theory. I grabbed the package from Benji and ran the rest of the way up the stairs. Door locked, I tore open the wrapper. Everything was there as promised—directions, plastic envelopes and labels. A week before I would have been ecstatic. But now it didn't matter. Dave hated me. But I'd paid for the damn thing, or should say, Chad had paid for it, so I had to go through with it. The door handle rattled.

"Brooke, open up."

"Benji, go away."

"But someone is here to see you."

I jammed my Panama back on my head, unlocked the door and peeked over the wrought iron railing. There, standing at the bottom of the staircase, was my old boyfriend Tyler Jensen. He looked as cute as ever. Pug nose, blond hair that stuck up any old way, and a crooked grin.

He looked up and waved.

"Why are you here?" I hissed, scampering down the stairs.

"I want to see you."

"No one wants to see me these days, Tyler. I'm persona non grata, or haven't you heard?"

"Well, actually, yeah. Can we talk somewhere private?"

I grabbed a jacket from the hall closet and led Tyler through the backyard. The air was cold and clean. It was almost like living in New Jersey.

"What do you want to talk to me about?" I asked once I had him far enough away from the house.

"I just wanted to see if you're okay."

"Why?"

"Because they're blaming you for the Surf's Up robbery."

"Let me guess who told you. Sudsy."

He shook his head. "Nope, Chad Roshbaum. He was hanging out at the Tastee Freeze showing off his new car."

"So, how did you two segue into talking about me?"

"Segue?"

"It means to move smoothly from one thing to another, Tyler. I guess I'm going to have to do a vocabulary list for you."

"Well, he made some crack about you and I busted him in the mouth."

"You hit Chad?"

"Yeah. I warned him if he didn't shut up I'd hit him."

"Oh, Tyler. You know violence never solves anything."

"Yes, but it sure as hell felt good."

I bit my lip to keep from laughing. "Thank you, that was very sweet. But promise me you won't hit anyone again. You don't want to get into trouble with the police."

Like me.

"I promise." He leaned forward for a kiss.

"Tyler, stop! What about Paige? Aren't you two going together?"

"No. That was over a week ago. I mean, she's nice and cute and all that, but all she ever talks about is the mall and Facebook. Compared to you, she's really boring."

I laughed.

"So, since you and Chad aren't together anymore, do you want to go with me again?"

His face was so serious and darling that I wanted to patent him and make Tyler dolls. "You want to go with me again, even after all that's happened?"

His face looked more serious than ever. "I know you'd never steal anything, because I know the real Brooke Bentley, and she's the most wonderful girl in Coral Cove."

"Oh, Tyler." I leaned forward to kiss him but stopped. "But there's one thing I have to tell you." I took off my Panama and shook my head.

"Omigod! Your hair! What happened to it?"

"I cut it all off."

"Why?"

"I'm not sure. I guess it was just cathartic or something."

Tyler looked mystified.

"Don't worry. I'll put it on your vocabulary list."

After a couple of yummy kisses, we walked to the front of the house where Tyler had left his bike. I watched him ride off, then sneaked back into the kitchen for a plate of spaghetti which I popped into the microwave.

I felt a little better. Partly because I love spaghetti, but mostly because Tyler had stood by me. And I'd treated him like dirt. I sniffled. Well, I'd never take that pug-nosed little darling for granted again.

But a full stomach and Tyler loving me didn't solve all of my problems. I still had the Surf Up's theft hanging over my head. *I wonder what Mr. Wilkins has found out?* Did the police have any clues? For all I knew, they weren't even looking. That left it up to me.

There was something else too, I realized once I was alone in my bedroom scrutinizing my new Joan of Arc look in the mirror. Tomorrow I'd have to make my debut at school sans hair. Good thing I hadn't gotten carried away and shaved my head. They would have expelled me for sure.

I lay awake imagining the next day. Wearing my Panama was out. They had rules about stuff like that. I guess because of gangs. But I couldn't imagine a gang running around in Panama hats, even though it would be incredibly cool. Maybe I could stay home sick. Actually, worrying about everything was *making* me sick. If only I was a bear and could go into hibernation.

Histrionics. That's the best vocab word to describe my mother when she popped into my bedroom the next morning and caught a good look at me.

"Brooke, what *have* you done?"

I sat up, grabbing for my Panama hat that lay on the end of the bed, but unfortunately Erskine was sleeping in it. "Well, I just thought it was time for a haircut."

"You call *that* a haircut?" She rushed over to run her fingers through what was left of my mane. "You look like Tom Sawyer."

"Is that good or bad?"

The answer must have been bad, because she threw herself on my duvet and burst into tears. "Your beautiful hair. Your beautiful hair."

At the sound of her sobs, Benji popped in. When he saw me, his face lit up like one of the Christmas lights our dad had strung up outside our house.

"Damn, your hair really looks killer, Brooke."

"Benji!" One scream from my mother and he was out the door.

I gazed at her, wondering how to proceed. "Mom, I was wondering, I feel kind of sick to my stomach, so can I stay home from school?"

"What a coincidence! I'm sick to my stomach, too. Sick that my daughter, who happens to have the most gorgeous hair in the entire world, chopped if off like she was cutting off the top of a carrot."

"It will grow fast. That's what the lady at Beautiful You Wigs told me."

She lifted her head from my pillow. "You sold your hair?"

"I gave it to her. I thought I should do something worthwhile. Because it's seems like I've been messing up a lot lately… and everyone thinks I'm such a loser."

My mom wiped a tear on the shirttail of her blouse, then put her arm around me. "You're not a loser, Brooke. You didn't steal those swimsuits, and the police will eventually find the people who did."

I nodded. As though on cue, the phone rang. My mom leaned over the nightstand and picked up the receiver. "Hello? Oh hello, Mr.

Wilkins. Oh, no! What do we do now? Yes, I understand. I'll tell her." She wasn't smiling when she hung up.

"What?" I asked. My question hung in the air.

My mother's eyes began to cloud up, like she was going to cry again. "Mr. Wilkins just got a list of the stolen inventory. There were three white Juicy Coutures. A small, a medium and a large."

Fear wrapped around my heart like a clump of seaweed pulling me down. Down, down to the murky bottom of the gulf.

"So, I suppose now the police are convinced the white Juicy that Greek detective found in the Green Lady was stolen from Surf's Up."

My mother nodded. "He said the State Attorney's Office is pushing the police to formally charge you. They're being pressured by a group that claims the law goes easier on rich kids."

"But, we're not rich."

"No, but some people think so."

It was my turn to bury my face in my pillow. After a few hysterical shrieks I lifted my head. "They're going to throw me into JDC, just like a criminal! I hear they don't even let you have your own hairbrush." I dove back into my pillow.

"Oh, Brooke." My mother patted the back of my practically hairless head.

"Nobody even cares that I'm innocent," I blubbered. "Nobody."

My mom pulled me up and looked into my eyes. "Listen, honey, your father and I care. And, we believe you, and we're not going to let you go to JDC, all right? We'll hire a private detective if we have to."

I nodded. *A private detective!* My life had turned into an episode of *Law and Order*.

When my mom left the room, I texted the same message to each of the Sisters.

Home sick. Meet @ Tastee Freeze 3:00pm 4 crucial meeting. C U Brooke

On the way to meet the Sisters, I swung by the post office to mail the DNA samples. I almost said *forget about it*. I mean, at this point I could care less about anybody's DNA. Or was it, *couldn't* care less? Whatever, I had to face it. It was just another one of my inane schemes. The kind of stuff that had gotten me into trouble over and over.

91

In my usual disguise of sunglasses and Panama, I arrived at the Tastee Freeze early. I was propped up against the wall like a catatonic (appropriate word for the day) when Tamara and Sudsy pulled up in Sudsy's mother's blue BMW.

"Well, the little capitalist goes for a milk shake," I sneered when she and Tamara sat down at the table. I was in another hellacious mood.

"Oh, can it," Sudsy answered. "I can't help it my mom has a Beemer. When I get my own car, it's going to be a VW. Something a little more proletarian."

I raised an eyebrow.

"Don't worry, Brooke. It's on your new list. I didn't have a chance to give it to you yesterday." She pushed a sheet of typewritten words across the table.

I took the list, crumpled it, and tossed it in the dirt. "Don't bother. I've been kicked off the vocabulary team. Besides, when they throw me into JDC, I'll probably learn a lot of exciting new words."

Tamara pulled her baseball cap down over her forehead and moved closer. "Girl, what makes you think you're going to JDC?"

I spent the next few minutes telling T and Sudsy about that morning's phone call from Mr. Wilkins. Sudsy got up to fly around the table to hug me.

"Brooke, when your parents hire a real honest to God detective, they're sure to find the guys who did it."

"They have to," Tamara chimed in, "because if they don't, those tough kids at JDC will make mincemeat out of you."

I whimpered and laid my head down on the sticky Tastee Freeze table.

Sudsy patted my shoulder. "Brooke is not going to JDC, Tamara, so knock it off."

There was silence. I could feel my friends' sympathetic stares. Finally, I lifted my head, my Panama tilted rakishly over one eye.

Tamara squinted at me. "You look different, girlfriend." She reached across the table and pulled off my hat. "Omigod!" Tamara and Sudsy's voices were almost in unison.

Sudsy was so surprised she knocked over her chocolate malt. "What the hell did you do?"

"Maybe Maria's dad got revenge with his Weed Wacker for that Homecoming gig," Tamara said. "Remember, he is their gardener."

"I did it," I said. "Don't ask me why, because I don't know."

Sudsy ran her fingers through what was left of my hair. "Obviously, it was a total act of rebellion. Maybe you'll start a new fad at school."

Tamara grimaced. "Yeah, right."

"Say, where's Maria?" I asked, changing the subject.

"She's working," Tamara said. "Besides, we're really not in the mood to see that particular Sister today. Suds and I aren't scheduled until Saturday."

"Well, at least you still have jobs."

Tamara looked startled. "Why, our hippie boss didn't fire you, did he?"

"No, but Mr. Wilkins advised my parents I shouldn't work until the cops find out who did it."

"Well, since we're still working, that must mean they don't think Sudsy and I had anything to do with the robbery."

It was as though a line had been drawn down the middle of the concrete Tastee Freeze table.

"So, in other words, I'm the scapegoat for this whole Maria deal." The words came out of my mouth like a croak.

Sudsy clicked her tongue.

"Look," Tamara began in a diplomatic tone, "we know you didn't steal anything, but it looks bad for you since the cops *did* find that Juicy bikini in your car."

"But," I added, "Paris Breck bought a white size 6-8 Juicy from me a couple of months ago, the time I called her an eponym. I remember, because I'd been lusting after that suit for weeks. She must have stashed it in my car some day when I parked in back of Surf's Up."

"How the hell are you going to prove it?" Leave it to Tamara to rain on my only sliver of hope. "We must have sold that same white Juicy to fifteen people."

"And," Tamara went on like a prosecuting attorney, "although we know you didn't swipe Dave's keys, you were the one who found them in the parking lot."

"T has a point," Sudsy said. "Just because Paris went into Dave's

93

office with him to make kissy-face, it doesn't prove she stole the keys."

I threw my head down on the sticky table again, covering my face with my hat.

Sudsy patted my hand like a mother trying to soothe a fractious (old vocab word) child. "Brooke, maybe you should just let the lawyer your parents hired figure it out. There's nothing Tamara and I can do."

"Yeah, and where does that leave me? Christmas vacation in JDC, that's where. And what about school? I'm sure everybody knows by now."

Sudsy blushed. "I only told Chad Roshbaum and he *already* knew. Mrs. Ethos told him."

"Great. Well, do me a favor, Suds. As long as you're blabbing everything, please tell the Gossip Girls that the police haven't charged me with anything." I got up and retreated to the refuge of the Green Lady.

"Chill out, Sister." Tamara's words followed me while I walked away. "Everything will be fine if you be cool and let the police handle it."

"Yeah, just be cool," Sudsy parroted.

But I didn't want to be cool. I was mad and I wanted to get even.

Okay, I was on my own. It didn't matter. Maybe when it came down to it, you're always alone in this world. I'd figure something out, but deep down I didn't have a clue. Maybe my reputation was ruined forever.

My mother let me stay home from school one day. It was really stretching it for her, but I guess she felt sorry for me. But even I knew I couldn't hide my Joan of Arc haircut forever.

"Are you going to be okay?" She appeared in the kitchen, her African safari nightgown flowing around her.

Deafened by the whirring of my mango/guava smoothie in the Vita Mix, I turned off the machine, poured the pinkish drink into a glass, and plunked down on a barstool. She swished over and sat down next to me.

"Do you feel better this morning?"

"I guess. I'm not the only girl who ever cut her hair. I just don't remember anyone cutting it this short."

"Actually, I'm getting used to it. It's good you have perfect features."

"Yeah, right." I wasn't in the mood for compliments.

In my Warrior Woman mode, I drove to school in semi disguise i.e. my Panama hat. I even wore it until I got to my locker. A quick look into the little mirror inside the door revealed a scared face. *Just fake it, Brooke. Be strong. No tears; remember Warrior Woman.*

It takes a lot to catch the Coral Cove Gossip Girls off guard, but I did that morning. Logan Lee and Paige Barton were holding court with some of their ladies in waiting when I sashayed past them in the hall.

Logan's super-fake smile cracked.

"Brooke, omigod! They cut your hair!" Paige shrieked, insinuating the Coral Cove cops had sheared me.

I shrugged.

"Do you like it?" Paige asked.

"Of course, I *like* it. It's the very latest thing. I read about boy cuts in the new issue of V*ogue* when I was out sick."

Paige made a moue. "I just got my new *Vogue* and I didn't read that."

"That's because I subscribe to the *European* issue, Paige. And seeing it's in French and you can barely speak English, how could you know?"

The entire ladies in waiting entourage giggled.

Considering everything, the day didn't go too bad. A few kids actually told me they liked my hair. I put on extra eye makeup just so no one would mistake me for a boy. Tyler sat with me at lunch and everything went fine except for a few lethal looks from Paige Barton.

Even Ms. Ethos was super nice, but she did look pretty waffled when I meandered in practically hairless. I was nice back, but aloof. I didn't want to be too easy. Sure, it wasn't her fault I was kicked off the Vocabulary Bee team, but she could have resigned in protest or something. She didn't have to just cave.

I didn't see Maria until school was over. I was at my locker when she sauntered by.

"Hi, Brooke," she said.

"Hi, yourself."

"Are you still mad at me?"

I looked at the face I'd known since pre-school and melted. She couldn't help it she was born clueless. "Sort of."

"I don't blame you. I'm mad at me too."

"Well, that would be a first."

The sarcasm (appropriate vocab word) was lost on Maria.

"T and Sudsy told me what's going on with the robbery. I just want you to know, even though they've pooped out, I'm here for you."

"You are?"

She nodded.

Hmm. I felt like I did when I agreed to let Benji help and he'd practically burned down the house. But Maria was better than no one.

"So what are we going to do?" Her eyes were wide with anticipation.

"Well…" I didn't want to admit I didn't have a plan. "I'm thinking about it."

As to what the plan would be, I was as clueless as Maria. But something would pop into my brain. It always did.

Chapter Thirteen

Christmas has always been my favorite holiday. Colored lights and a blowup Santa in the yard, tinsel on the tree, my mom baking sugar cookies, and my greedy little brother foraging for presents.

But this year it was pretty dismal. I mean, with the Surf's Up robbery hanging over my head, I'd felt about as festive as Scrooge. And it only took a couple of seconds Christmas Eve morning to remember, even though I was pure as the driven snow, I was still persona non grata when it came to the general consensus of Coral Cove.

I spent the morning wrapping presents in my bedroom. As a gesture of goodwill, my dad resumed my allowance, giving me two back weeks so I could buy stuff for Christmas. I was just wrapping Benji's gift when he barged in with Erskine.

"Benji, I swear to God. You are the biggest snoop."

"I am not snooping. I just wanted to give you this before Mom saw it."

He handed me an envelope. The letters C.T.L were on the upper left hand corner. It could only be one thing—the results of the DNA test! I looked at Benji. "I'm afraid to open it."

"Here, let me. I love to open stuff." Benji tore open the envelope, then scanned the letter. "I don't understand what they're saying."

I took the letter from his chubby paw and sat down on the bed with Erskine.

Subject A. Subject B. Subject C. Results findings. 98.99999 conclusive. I collapsed on my bed.

"I don't believe it. I don't believe it!"

"What don't you believe?"

97

Laura Kennedy

"Benji, if I tell you, you have to promise to keep it a secret. So help you God."

"I promise."

"Okay. According to this, it says they're 98.99999 percent sure that Dave, subject B, is Mom's (subject A) dad."

"Yippee! New surfboard here I come. So why do you look all weird and funny?"

"Because, it also says subject C is *not* subject A's mother."

"I don't get it."

"Subject C, Grandma Donnie, isn't Mom's real mom!"

Benji looked like he was going to cry. "So, does that make us illegitimate or what?"

"Of course not."

"Well, then does that make Mom—"

"Benji, please. It just means she was adopted."

"Do you think she knows it?"

"I don't know, but I think she would have told us."

"Poor Mom."

"Now, Benji, you have to promise. *Do not* ruin Christmas and our mother's entire life by telling her something she probably doesn't want to know."

"I promise I won't say a word. Poor little thing. Probably tossed in a dumpster or something."

Benji and I spent the rest of Christmas Eve being really nice to our mother. I mean, after dinner we filled the dishwasher and put the food away in Tupperware. I even washed the lasagna dish.

Mom was bewildered. "Gee, you kids are so sweet. I guess you're hoping for something great tomorrow." She nodded to the fireplace where she'd hung our stockings. There was even one for Erskine.

"No, we just love and appreciate you," Benji answered, "because some little kids don't have mothers."

I gave him a little kick in the ankle.

Dad beamed. "Well, you do have a really special mother, that's for sure." He leaned over and gave her a kiss. Not his usual chicken peck, but a real mushy one, just like Tyler and me.

Later Tyler came over to give me a present, but my mind was back at Woodstock.

"You didn't like the locket?" he asked. We were alone in the den. "Maybe I should have put your picture in it instead of mine."

"No, no. I love wearing a picture of you, Tyler. I guess I'm just tired from everything that's been going on."

After Tyler left, I sat in the dark looking at the lights on our tree, remembering one of Grandma Donnie's cornball expressions. *Leave well enough alone.* Well, per usual, I hadn't left well enough alone. I'd found out Dave was my grandpa. I'd also found out Grandma Donnie *wasn't* Mom's real mother, which meant Grandma Donnie *wasn't* my real grandmother! Then who *was* my real grandmother?

Don't start, Brooke, I warned myself. *You've done enough damage.*

Christmas Day. Eggnog and waffles for breakfast. Christmas church service on the bayou. And Christmas dinner with Grandma Donnie.

When Dave showed up at the door, you could have knocked me over with my new rain stick, a present from Benji. Actually for a second, I felt like knocking Dave off the steps with the rain stick.

"Hi, Brooke," he said. "Merry Christmas."

He wore a white dress shirt, a red ribbon tied around his singed ponytail and an embarrassed look.

"Hi, Dave. Come on in."

"Hope you're not mad about the stuff that went down at the store. I never told the cops you did it, just that you found the keys. I guess they drew their own conclusions. They told me I shouldn't let you work until they found out who really robbed the place."

I thought you're supposed to be innocent until proven guilty. But I didn't say it.

Dave stared at Erskine who was rubbing against his leg. "So, to make it up to you, I have something in the van."

I followed Dave to the front driveway to his VW. It was yellow and old and had about a million dents he'd tried to hide with red peace signs and white doves. A ratty looking *Impeach Nixon* bumper sticker peered out at me from inside the back window.

"Well, here it is." He pulled open the side door.

I blinked, not believing my eyes. I blinked again. There in front of me was a yellow Honey surfboard decorated with pink and red hibiscus.

"Do you like it?"

"Omigod, Dave. Is it mine?"

He nodded.

"I don't know what to say except…thank you. Thank you so much!"

"Holy cow! Dave gave *you* a board when you don't even, like surf?" Benji's sonar had kicked in and he stood beside me.

"I'm going to teach her," Dave said. "The waves around here really suck, but we can all go to the east coast some weekend."

Benji looked majorly bummed.

"And I'll teach you too, bro. Maybe next year you'll find a board in your stocking."

Benji let out a yelp coinciding with the arrival of Grandma Donnie who'd just pulled into the drive, looking very Christmas-y in her red SL. Enjoying her entrance, she made the most of stretching her legs when she got out of the car.

"Hi, Hot Shot," she said giving me a kiss on the cheek. "Staying out of trouble?"

"Trying," I answered.

"Well, remember what Yoda said. 'Do or do not. There is no try.' "

Benji and I gave each other a look. Since when was Grandma Donnie into *Star Wars?*

We sat around the living room after dinner, opening presents. I kept looking at Dave, remembering how just this past Thanksgiving I'd thought Donnie was the love of his life. No wonder he hadn't recognized her. Well, maybe that Denise chick was somewhere out there waiting for him.

We opened our presents, watching Erskine go crazy in the wrapping paper. I guess that's why nobody noticed when Benji disappeared, reappearing with a mangled present wrapped in Santa paper and a ton of tape. He handed it to Dave.

"Well, thank you, Benji. That was very thoughtful."

That Benji. Already buttering Dave up for next year's surfboard.

We sat there. Me, Mom, Dad, Grandma Donnie and Benji, watching Dave in that polite sort of way you do when someone's opening a gift. He fumbled with the mess of tape until he tore open the package. A package that held a huge white T-shirt. I read the lettering on the back and gasped. There, in about 96 point cap, was the following damning message—*The World's Best Grandpa.*

"Well, this is just great, bro," Dave said, oblivious of the time bomb he held.

I leaped to my feet, wildly grabbing for the T-shirt. But I was too late. Dave turned the shirt around and looked at the message.

"Grandpa?" The word came out as a squeak.

I forced a smile and grabbed Benji by the arm. "He just thinks of you as a grandpa, don't you, Benji?"

"Yeah, especially now since I found out you really are."

My terrified eyes shot to Grandma Donnie whose face was cadaver-white in spite of her Lancôme bronzer.

"For God's sake, Benji, what are you talking about?" she yowled.

I dragged my little brother toward the kitchen. He struggled in my arms, turning his bowling-ball-head to glare at me. "Oww! That hurt."

"Benji, I need to talk to you alone, please."

"Why are you mad at me?" he bellowed. "You never said I couldn't tell the part about Dave."

My new grandpa was on his feet, making a dash through the open sliding glass door to the pool, most likely for an encore on-fire-Thanksgiving-day leap, except maybe this time to drown himself.

"The kid's crazy," Grandma Donnie said, staggering to her feet. "Don't pay any attention to him."

My mother looked a holiday green. "All right, Benji, what's going on?"

Benji escaped my grip and took a deep breath, like he was going to recite the Gettysburg Address or something. He had everyone's attention. I waited for the words to come out of his traitorous yap, like a character in the denouement scene in a Dickens' novel.

"Well, to begin with, Brooke sent away to this lab place. She took Dave's old Band-Aid, and Mom's hair, and Donnie's cigarette butt. They tested them and found out Dave's our grandpa. Kind of neat, right?"

Grandma Donnie grabbed at her heart and sank back against the couch. "I need a drink."

"I'll get it," my dad said and leaped to our bar. By then Dave had staggered back to the planter's chair. No one uttered a syllable. We sat in silence while the adults all drank. After draining her whiskey and Coke, Donnie turned to face us.

"Well, I guess it's time I told the truth," she said. "Especially to you, Barbie."

"You and Dave?" my mother croaked. She'd almost drained her whiskey and Coke too, so a little color had come back into her face.

Donnie shook her head. "No. Dave and my best friend Denise."

"Denise?" Dave bellowed. "Denise from Woodstock? That's why you look so familiar!"

"Yes, Dave. I was the friend who was with her. It was August of 1969 and Denise and I were nineteen. We heard about an outdoor concert in Woodstock, New York and decided to go. All the big rock stars were going to be there—Jimi Hendricks, Janis Joplin, Blood Sweat and Tears." She was like one of those talking windup dolls that won't stop. "So we took off in my old Plymouth. As soon as we got there, we hooked up with a couple of guys—me with a kid named Dean, and Denise with a blonde surfer from California named Dave."

Dave was on his feet, like he was in a daze. "Omigod!" he kept saying. "Omigod!"

"Dean and I fell hard for each other, and two months later we got married. It was just about the time Denise found out she was pregnant. But Dave had gone back to California and she didn't know how to find him. She was afraid to tell her folks, so she moved in with Dean and me."

I looked at my mother. Big fat tears tumbled down her cheeks. "Why didn't you tell me?" she asked. "Why didn't you tell me?"

Donnie ignored her and kept on talking. "Denise lived with us until she gave birth. Six weeks later she moved to Las Vegas, leaving the baby with us. It wasn't long before Dean left, too. I guess raising a baby that wasn't his was too much. I never saw either one of them again."

"Oh, Mom," my mother said for the umpteenth time. "Why didn't you tell me?"

"I was afraid. Afraid they'd take you away." Tears streamed down her face. By then we were all crying.

"What ever happened to the other lady?" Benji sniffled. Thank God he hadn't said the *real* mother.

"We kept in touch, but five years ago my Christmas card came back. I knew something was terribly wrong so I went on the Internet and found Denise's obituary in the newspaper. She'd died in a car crash."

Christmas ended early. Drained, I staggered off to bed at nine. I didn't have an ounce of tears left. In my room, I thought about all that had happened. I'd found a grandfather and lost a grandmother. But I guess having a family is a lot more than just DNA.

I wanted to be mad at Benji, but couldn't. I mean, maybe it was a good thing that he'd told. Grandma Donnie had been carrying this secret around her whole life. And Dave had been looking for Denise *his* whole life.

I thought of the Surf Shop Sisters. Did the four of us have that kind of friendship? The kind of friendship like Donnie's and Denise's? Sudsy, Tamara and I had been there for Maria, but it had only gotten us in trouble. And now when it came to being there for me, Sudsy and Tamara had bailed out. It looked like the only one who knew how to be a good friend was me. I guess it ran in the family.

From my bedroom window I watched the red and green Christmas lights on the palms trees in the front yard. Things would never be the same again, I realized. Never, ever. Especially for Mom and Donnie and Dave.

But what about me? Now that everyone in the family was all worked up about who was and wasn't who, did anybody really care I might end up in the slammer?

Chapter Fourteen

I never knew what anti-climactic meant until the morning after Christmas. It was like the end of the world— Benji slinking around the house like a lizard; my dad shooting daggers at both of us; me living in terror the cops might knock on the door any second and drag me to JDC in my new True Religion jeans; and my mom languishing in bed like Madame Bovary.

I sneaked a peek at her where she lay staring at the ceiling fan. Her black silk Oriental pajamas were perfect for the languishing role. Tea and toast on the nightstand, she seemed mesmerized by the twirling blades. I didn't blame her. It would be pretty shocking to find out the person you'd call Mom your entire life wasn't your real mother.

I skulked down stairs to the living room. Erskine rubbed against my leg. I was grateful for the attention since no one had uttered a syllable to me since Benji had pulled the pin on the hand grenade that destroyed Christmas. I looked at the damning T-shirt where it lay balled up in the planter's chair, like it carried the bubonic plague.

Poor shirt. Maybe it would just lie there forever, like Miss Havishams' wedding dress in *Great Expectations,* until it disintegrated into yellow dust. I thought of the future longingly, wishing it were here. I picked up the World's Best Grandpa tee and jammed it into my new Kate Spade hobo purse, my Christmas present from Grandma Donnie, and ran out the front door.

By Monday Christmas was nothing but a traumatic memory. With no school, there was nothing left to do but focus on proving my innocence. Sure, the Coral Cove cops hadn't charged me with robbery yet, but the old holiday spirit only lasts so long, which didn't leave much time to prove Paris Breck was the real Surf's Up thief. And it looked like I'd have to do it alone, except for Maria. Even the Lone Ranger had Tonto.

An hour later I pulled around the corner of Dodecanese just as Maria strolled out of Surf's Up. Decked out in a white blouse, tangerine jeans and a teal scarf around her head, she looked like she'd just run away from a band of Gypsies. Seeing me, she jumped into the car.

"What's with the scarf?"

"I wanted to create a different look for the New Year, like you did with your hair, but not so drastic. So where are we going?"

"Point Omega. That's where Paris Breck lives. We're going to follow her when she comes out."

Maria nodded. One thing about Maria, she had faith in me, unlike Sudsy who would have asked a million questions, and Tamara who would have had a million objections.

It was a gorgeous day. The kind of winter day Floridians like to take pictures of and send to people up north, just to rub it in. We had the top down, and for a couple of minutes I felt almost happy. Except for the dark cloud hanging over me and my Panama. So, it was a chilly sixty degrees. I could take it.

We parked under a queen palm across the street from Point Omega. Not to be so conspicuous, I put the top up.

"Okay, here's the deal. I staked out this spot for half-an-hour before I picked you up, and Paris never came out. And unless she left during the ten minutes it took to get you, she's still in there."

"What if she never comes out?"

"She has to sometime."

"True."

Thankfully, Maria had no more questions because I wasn't in the mood for logic.

We sat in silence. Me, eating carob covered almonds and reading *Seventeen*, dreaming of the Dooney & Bourke Dreamsicle-print hobo purse I'd buy if I ever had a regular allowance again or returned to work; Maria, texting and twirling her Gypsy scarf.

Maria stopped mid-twirl. "Brooke, here she comes."

I stared through the window. Wearing huge sunglasses and dressed in red like a she-devil was Paris Breck. She hopped into her Caddy and started the engine. Maria and I popped down in the Green Lady.

"Don't follow too close," Maria warned after we'd popped up. I let a car slip between us, then pulled out, keeping the Green Lady back far enough so Paris wouldn't spot us when we followed her through the gate.

"Don't worry. I've seen enough TV shows to know how to tail someone."

Maria tightened her scarf. "So what are we going to do when she does stop some place?"

"I don't know. I just want to see if she does anything suspicious."

From Gulf View Drive, the Caddy turned on Spring Bayou, then onto U.S. 19.

Maria sucked her finger, a holdover from pre-school. "Hope she's not going to Tampa or something."

"I'll follow her to Tallahassee if I have to."

But a tour of the State Capitol wasn't in our future, but a red light was. We watched the back of Paris' Caddy as it disappeared up 19.

"You should have run it," Maria said.

"Couldn't risk it. They're practically printing pictures of me to hang in the post office already."

"Now we'll never find her."

It must have been the longest red light in history with one of those left turn arrows gigs thrown in. When it finally turned green, I flew down 19, trying to spot Double Bubble on Wheels.

"Keep looking, Maria. She might have turned in some place already."

We drove as far as Sunset Point, but no Caddy.

"Maybe we should turn around," Maria said. "I don't think she went this far."

"I didn't see her turn."

We'd driven about a mile when Maria began squealing. "Brooke, stop! There's her car." I made a sharp right into a little strip mall. There sitting like a prop in an old Elvis movie was the infamous pink Caddy.

"Where do you think she went? Maria asked, surveying the row of small shops.

Hmm. Guitar store, electronics place, Pizza Hut, nail salon. "Well, since I don't think she's musical or geeky, I'd say—"

"Nail shop!" Maria crowed.

I parked the Green Lady around the corner and Maria and I loped to the nail salon. Heaven's Gate Nails. The windows were painted a no-see-through gold. We sauntered in. A life-size Buddha stood in the entry next to a big plastic Santa. A middle-aged Vietnamese lady stood behind the counter.

"May I help you?" she asked.

"Well, actually, I'm looking for someone. My aunt. She has red hair, but some days it's blonde."

"Client information strictly confidential."

I heard a voice and glanced down the hallway. There stood Paris and Tiffany. I nudged Maria until she looked, too. So Tiffany had met Mommy for an afternoon of bonding. Yes!

"Well, I was thinking about having a pedicure," I began.

The lady brightened. "Ah, you read about special fish pedicure?"

I nodded.

"Garra rufa, Doctor Fish. Very popular."

Maria and I giggled.

"I explain. Tiny fish put in tank in private booth where soak feet. Bite off dead skin and make feet oh so soft."

I bit my lip. "Is it safe? I mean, they don't get carried away and bite off your toes or anything."

"Oh, no. Very safe."

"How much?"

Thirty dollar half-hour. Fifty hour."

"Could you excuse us for a minute?"

Maria and I stepped outside. She looked worried. "That's a lot of money just to eavesdrop."

"Yeah, but maybe they'll say something incriminating."

"All right, how much money do you have?"

"Ten dollars."

"I'll pay the rest. After all, I owe you." She handed me a twenty.

Maria was right. She did owe me. And thirty bucks plus a tip to the carp was getting off easy considering all I'd been through.

The lady was busy leaning against the counter when Maria and I reappeared.

"Okay, I'll do it," I said.

I paid and Maria and I followed her down a hallway to an emerald door that opened into a large room. There, separated by heavy pink curtains, were six compartments. The lady pulled aside a curtain marked number two. We peeked in.

"Each customer own tank and fish. Complete private."

I stopped and listened. A few compartments down I could make out Paris' phony voice.

"There robe if you like to make self comfortable."

"No thanks, I'll just roll up my jeans. But just one little thing," I said. "I don't like this booth. I want number four. It's my lucky number."

"Lucky number?"

It's good I don't understand Vietnamese, because I'm sure whatever the Heaven's Gate lady mumbled wasn't virtuous.

"This okay?" she asked once she led us to compartment number four.

I listened for Paris's voice through the curtain. "Perfect. Absolutely perfect."

"Look at those fish!" Maria squealed when the lady left. "Are you really going to let them chew on your toes?"

"Shh," I whispered, taking off my shoes. "Don't talk. Just listen."

I rolled up the cuffs of my white jeans and put my feet into the cool tank of water. The fish raced to me like I was a plate of hors d'oeuvres.

"Omigod!" I laughed.

"What's it like?" Maria asked.

"It tickles so much I can hardly stand it." I giggled again. Maria started laughing, too. "Shh, we need to listen."

"I don't know." It was Paris. "I should probably get another car."

"Yeah, Alyse. The Caddy's got a lot of miles."

"Alyse, who's that?" I mouthed to Maria.

Tiffany continued. "Besides, your car is too easy to recognize."

"I need to, but new cars are expensive."

"Why should you care? We've got plenty of money."

Maria and I looked at each other and gave a thumbs up. God, if I could only record their conversation.

Tiffany shrieked. Apparently, one of the garra rufa hadn't read Emily Post and had taken a bigger bite than what was polite.

"So, how much longer does this Doctor Fish gig last?" Tiffany said when she'd calmed down. "This is pretty damn weird."

"Lady? Excuse me, but we have problem." It was the voice of the lady manager who'd apparently entered their cubicle.

"A problem?" Paris parroted in her phony voice.

"Credit card turned down. No good."

"That's impossible. There must have been some kind of mistake." The cool had gone out of Paris' voice.

"Okay, then I call owner."

"Alyse, let's get out of here before they call the cops."

"You no go. You pay first!"

There was the sound of a struggle, a splash, and more screaming, first in Vietnamese, then English.

"Help! Help! I no can swim!"

Maria looked alarmed. "My, God! They've tossed her in the pool!"

"I doubt she'll drown in three feet of water, but you better help bail her out. I'm going after Paris."

"Be careful, Brooke. She's bigger and crazier than you are."

Bigger, yes. Crazier, no. I grabbed my purse and galloped out of the booth into the hallway. I couldn't let Paris get away.

I ran out the front door. Paris was ahead of me, already backing the Caddy out of her parking space. I'd just given up the idea of blocking her with the Green Lady when a humungous Pepsi truck pulled up behind her. A good-looking guy in shorts got out and started unloading. He had great legs and an attitude.

"You're blocking my way, you moron!" Paris yelled.

"Moron yourself, lady. I'll be out of here in a minute."

Thank you, God. I was just retrieving Detective Stavrakidis' business card from my purse when Maria jumped into the car.

"I'm calling Detective Stavrakidis," I said. "Now we know Paris is crooked."

"Do you think he'll come?"

Laura Kennedy

"He said to call if I need him and God knows I need him now."

I punched in the number. A dispatcher answered, telling me he was in the field and she'd have him call me.

There was a slam. We looked up to catch the Pepsi guy getting back into his truck. Behind him an impatient Paris gunned her engine while he pulled out. But before she could move, I pulled the Green Lady behind the Caddy, blocking her.

I got out of the convertible, Maria at my heels. What was I going to do now? I wasn't sure. All I knew was there was something weird going on.

Paris put her head out the window. "What are you doing? Is there something wrong with you? Get your car out of my way, you little stalker."

"Miss Breck, I'd like to ask you a couple of questions first. It will only take a few minutes."

"Well, this will only take a minute," she said, throwing the Caddy into reverse and slamming into the Green Lady. I watched in horror as her head bounced around like a bobble head doll. Omigod! She'd totaled my car!

"Now, will you move?" she screamed.

"No," I yelled back. "Not until you tell me if you planted a Juicy Couture suit in my car."

She answered by slamming the Caddy into the Green Lady again.

Maria started to cry. I felt like crying too, but forced myself to stay calm.

I was just wondering what to do next when my cell rang. It was Detective Stavrakidis.

"Could you please come, right now?" My voice was only semi-hysterical. "Paris Breck is destroying my convertible."

"Who's Paris Breck?"

"A suspicious customer. I think she knows something about the robbery. I've blocked her with my car."

"Where are you?"

"Heaven's Gate Nail Salon. It's in a strip mall just south of Sunrise Drive on U.S 19."

"Be there in a minute."

An aqua and white squad car beat him to it. I was never happier to see the cops in my entire life. There were two of them, one African-American, one white.

"So what's going on?" the black cop asked. His nametag said Officer Johnson.

Now out of the Caddy, Paris was in rare form. "Officer, this little juvenile delinquent blocked my car and I can't get out."

Hmm. That was the second time I'd been called a juvenile delinquent.

"So, is that why you backed your vehicle into her?" Officer Johnson asked.

Paris looked flustered. "She provoked it when she blocked me. Aren't there laws against that? And," she took a breath, "she followed me into the salon where I was getting a fish pedicure and molested me."

The other cop grinned.

"Ma'am?" It was obvious Officer Johnson had never heard of garra rufa.

If he needed an explanation, one was on the way, because just that second the door of the salon flew open and the Asian lady and her daughter came flying out. They were both yelling in Vietnamese.

Officer Johnson held up his hand. "Whoa, hold on, ladies, please. Just calm down and tell me, in English, what happened." He took a small pad and pencil from his pocket.

The younger woman spoke first. "Well, to begin with these girls came into our salon..." Blah, blah, blah. She never took a breath until she was through.

The white cop motioned Maria and me away. "Girls, could I talk to you a minute?"

I parked my injured Green Lady in the shade and walked back to the officer. Maria and I were giving him our version of the story when Detective Stavrakidis pulled up in an unmarked car. I could have kissed him, even if he was like thirty-five.

"Okay, Brooke, Maria, what's up?"

The second cop left and I proceeded to tell the detective what was going on, including the part about the carp pedicure. "So, I think Paris Breck had something to do with the robbery. She bought a swimsuit just like the one you found in my convertible."

"I'll run her tag, but it doesn't sound like you have any proof. It looks like the only ones in trouble are you two. The owner of the salon could charge you girls with criminal mischief."

"Criminal mischief?" Maria looked like she wanted to bolt.

Detective Stavrakidis walked over to the Caddy. Paris was at the goo-goo-eyed stage with Officer Johnson. As though a young good-looking guy like him would be interested in someone that old.

The detective cleared his throat. "Ma'am, your license and registration, please."

"But officer, I haven't done anything."

"Ma'am?"

Paris reached into her car for her purse, returning with her registration and license. "I don't know why you're harassing me when this girl is the one who is obviously in the wrong."

"Ma'am, have you had anything to drink?"

"Drink? Drink? I wish I had something to drink after dealing with a reprobate (new word to look up) like you."

Detective Stavrakidis' jaw clenched. Apparently, reprobate wasn't a compliment. "Open the trunk, ma'am."

"How dare you search my car without a warrant?" Paris yelled. A ghostly white crept over her pancake make-up face. "Why aren't you opening *her* trunk? She's the one who broke the law."

The detective remained unmoved. Paris turned and walked back to the Caddy and slipped behind the wheel. But instead of popping the trunk, she gunned the engine and backed up, practically running us over.

It was like being in a movie, it all happened so fast. Paris screeching through the parking lot. Detective Stavrakidis and the cops hopping in their cars and peeling after her.

"Come on, Maria." Wide-eyed, we ran to my convertible and jumped in. I turned the key in the ignition and a puff of smoke wafted out from under the hood.

"Come on, Green Lady. Don't fail me now."

"They're headed south," Maria yelled.

We followed the sound of screaming sirens and a path of cars that pulled over to let us pass.

"Are we going to get in trouble for chasing them?" Maria asked, buckling her seat belt.

"I think the cops are too busy to care about us. Besides, I don't think the Caddy's going to be able to outrun them."

Two blocks later they were nowhere in sight.

"Where did they go?"

"I think Paris cut through the Walmart parking lot."

I made a quick right turn. There, dodging shopping carts and Saturday afternoon shoppers, was Paris' pink Caddy trailed by Coral Cove's finest. In seconds the cops were out of their cars and Paris Breck was spread eagled on the ground.

I parked the Green Lady and Maria and I ran over.

"It's all a terrible mistake," Paris wailed. "I was traumatized."

I guess cops are used to seeing a lot of traumatized people, because Detective Stavrakidis didn't answer. Instead he grabbed Paris' keys from the ignition and walked to the back of the Caddy and popped the trunk. He peered in and took out a small cardboard box that he opened.

"Well, well, well. Look what we've got here."

Maria and I peeked, too. "What are they?" I asked.

"Blank American Express cards. Oh, just a minute. A couple of them have been encoded. *James A. Watson, Jr., Cynthia Rehnquist, Stewart W. Holmes.*

"You mean they're stolen?" Maria squealed. By now her Gypsy bandana was over one eye. "Where did she get them?"

"On the street. She's probably got a replicating machine at home she bought for fifty or sixty grand."

"But, doesn't the credit card company know the cards are no good?" I asked.

"Eventually, but it takes a while. Meanwhile, thousands of dollars of merchandise have been purchased with fake plastic."

"Do you see anything else?" I held my breath.

Detective Stavrakidis lifted a corner of the blanket. Peeking out was a bit of blue and green. He reached in and pulled out a brand new Juicy Couture swimsuit, Surf's Up tags and all. "Is this what you're looking for?"

He rummaged around again, coming up with three more Juicys and three Aaron Changs.

I let out a yell.

Detective Stavrakidis grinned. "Of course, we'll have to check them out against the stolen merchandise list, but—"

"But?" I cut in.

"Finding this stuff makes things look good for you, Brooke."

Paris Breck *was* the Surf's Up thief and now they could prove it!

Maria and I jumped in the Green Lady and limped away. The engine made a terrible grinding noise and smoke poured from under the hood.

I looked at Maria. "I guess I need to call my dad and have him meet me at Joe's Body Shop."

"Yeah, but first, I think we should go to the Tastee Freeze to celebrate. You were great, Brooke. You never wimped out."

"You weren't too shabby yourself, Maria. But can I take a rain check on the malt? I'm exhausted."

She nodded and adjusted her Gypsy scarf. "You know, I was thinking, maybe you should be a detective someday. I mean, you knew Paris Breck was a criminal. Like it was instinct."

Hmm. Instinct. Well, right now my instincts told me to go home and sleep for like a year. I dropped Maria off, then crawled in the direction of Porpoise Drive.

I coaxed my convertible into the garage. By then there was so much smoke coming out from under the hood, I felt like I was sitting in the middle of a volcano.

In the kitchen, my parents sat at the counter. Even Benji and Erskine were there.

"I tried to get you on your cell, but you didn't answer," my mother said, getting up from a barstool.

"I guess so much was going on I didn't hear it."

My dad looked really happy, like he'd just gotten a big refund from the IRS. "Detective Stavrakidis called and told us what happened."

"I hope you're not mad about the Green Lady. I mean, she backed into me."

Benji leaped up, ran into the garage, yowled, and rushed back. "God, you really creamed your car, didn't you?"

My mom shook her head. "Benji, please. We're just thankful

Brooke's okay."

My dad stared at my soggy jeans. "What happened to you?"

"It's kind of a long story. Can I change first?"

The phone rang and my mom picked it up. I gathered it was good news, because when she hung up she was one big grin.

"Mr. Wilkins just had a call from Detective Stavrakidis, too."

"And?" my father asked.

"This Paris Breck woman confessed she's the head of a shoplifting ring. She's also admitted stealing Dave's keys, making a duplicate, and giving it to some guys who robbed Surf's Up."

So that was it! "She must have thrown Dave's keys in the dirt outside of Surf's Up so one of us would find them and look guilty.

It was my dad's turn. "Probably the same day she stashed that swimsuit in Brooke's convertible."

My heart was doing a samba. "So does that mean I'm cleared?"

My mom smiled. "Mr. Wilkins said the police have completely dismissed you as a suspect."

I rushed into my mother's arms. In a second my dad's arms were around both of us.

"Thank God it's over." And if I'd looked up, I think I would have seen my father cry for the first time.

After an emotionally satisfying dinner of spaghetti and meatballs, I took a long bubble bath. I felt so light and carefree, it was all I could do not to fall asleep and slip down the drain. It was like all that huge clump of seaweed had been cut from around my heart.

Okay, so maybe I hadn't really been tied up with seaweed, but I may as well have been. Everyone in Coral Cove thought I was a thief and a liar headed for JDC, both Tyler and Chad had broken up with me, I'd been kicked off the Vocabulary Bee, hacked off my hair, and my name had become an anathema, which is just a fancy word for mud. But none of that mattered now. The only thing that really mattered was that everyone would know I was innocent and I could just be me again.

I put on a nightshirt and crawled into bed. Propped up against my pillows, I turned on my laptop. Soon I'd sent three short e-mails into cyberspace.

To the three best friends in the universe. Here's what I think you should know about life—

Maria: To have freedom, U must first learn how to handle it.

Tamara: It takes more than nice stuff to make U happy.

Sudsy: Real beauty isn't just a # on the bathroom scale, it's what's inside.

And what have I learned? I wondered. Probably that when you put your friends first, your life can turn into a major nightmare. What I hadn't known, is that if you want people to like and respect you, you have to respect yourself first.

I switched off my laptop, but before turning off the light, I picked up Sudsy's replacement vocabulary list to see what my new word was for the following day.

Copacetic—excellent; when everything is going well. It was the perfect word to describe my life, almost.

Chapter Fifteen

Riding with the top down in my dad's borrowed Mustang, I felt practically human. So, it was a chilly sixty degrees. I could take it. Driving aimlessly, I surrendered and let the car choose the way.

I parked in front of Surf's Up and got out. Christmas music drifted through the front door. *Grandma got run over by a reindeer*. Dave probably wished Grandma Donnie had been run over by a reindeer. In fact, he probably wished we'd *all* been run over.

It seemed like a gazillion years since I'd been in the shop. Scattered around the shop, the Sisters looked like figures in Madame Tussauds Wax Museum. Dave glanced up from the cash register. I gave a weak wave, wondering what possessed me to show up at the last place in the world I wanted to be.

Maria smiled. The other little copycats smiled, too. "Hi, how was Christmas?" Sudsy asked, as the Sisters sashayed over. Somehow I had the feeling they sensed something was up.

"Oh, good. Dave gave me a yellow Honey surfboard."

"We know," Tamara answered. "We're the ones who picked it out."

"How were your Christmases?" I asked.

"Wonderful!" Maria answered. "Maybe I forgot to tell you, but Anthony sent me an engagement ring!"

"An engagement ring?"

"Yeah," Tamara said, jumping in. "I saw it. It's about the size of a grain of salt."

I frowned. "T, that's not nice."

"It's okay," Maria said. "I've already sent it back to him."

"Your parents wouldn't let you keep it?"

117

She shook her head. "No, I didn't want it. I'm over Anthony."

"What?" I said, remembering the cold night I'd spent camped out in the Don Carlos parking lot.

She nodded. "I need someone who really cares about me and is more ambitious. I mean, he doesn't even want to go to college. Now I know why my parents wouldn't let me date him. I guess I don't always make the best decisions."

I slapped my head like I was in a V-8 commercial on TV. If there had ever been an understatement in Surf Shop Sister history, this was it.

"Guess what?" Sudsy asked as I peeled my paw off my forehead.

"I've lost four pounds and wasn't even trying."

"You did?"

"Yeah, I got this incredible positive thinking book as an early Christmas present from Aunt Sophia. It's all about, you know…"

"Positive thinking," Tamara interjected.

I bit my lip to keep from laughing.

Sudsy shot T a scathing look. "It teaches you about learning to love yourself for who you really are. As soon as I stopped worrying about what the Gossip Girls and their ladies in waiting think about me, good stuff started to happen."

"Like what?" I asked.

"Like she and Chad Roshbaum are going together," Maria said.

I turned to Sudsy. I felt like doing another V-8 slap, but my brain couldn't take it. *Chad broke up with me to go with Sudsy?*

Sudsy looked smug. "Yeah, the new confident me envisioned Chad liking me, and the very next day he and his new silver convertible showed up at my house."

Maria beamed. "Chad told Sudsy she's the smartest girl he's ever met."

I raised my eyebrows. "Well, I'm really happy you *finally* have a boyfriend," I said, putting more emphasis on finally than was nice.

"And what about your Christmas?" I asked, turning to T.

"Well, Jamal came over Christmas Eve. He gave me a gorgeous yellow cashmere sweater. And, we agreed to do something really important when we graduate from law school."

"Get married and get killer six-figure jobs with some Fortune 500?"

Sudsy guessed.

"Partially," Tamara answered. "Go to law school and get killer jobs at a legal clinic in Miami."

"But, what about the expensive clothes, and the Jaguar, and all the other stuff you've been lusting for since you read your first *Town and Country* magazine?" I asked. "You're not going to make big bucks at a legal clinic."

"That can wait. Jamal made me realize there are a lot of people behind bars because they didn't get decent legal help. I guess Jamal and I got inspired by President Obama or something."

"God! Then you'll both get involved in politics and you'll be just like Michelle Obama," Maria squealed. "And when Jamal's elected president, I'll come and work for him as his press secretary."

Tamara did a neck roll. "Jamal, hell. I'm the one who's going to be president."

"Customers, girls," Dave's voice cut through our laughter. Seconds later the Sisters floated over to the trio of fresh meat.

I stood there, trying to digest the words spoken the past five minutes. A rejected diamond ring, a self-help book, and a president; the lives of my three BFFs had changed forever.

"Well, I guess I'll be leaving," I announced to the blowup Santa Claus on the counter. "Just came by to wish everyone a Merry Christmas." *No you didn't, you little liar,* Santa seemed to say. *You came by to see Dave.*

I inched toward the door, but Dave cut me off, a box of sunblock in his arms. He looked terrible, like he hadn't gotten any sleep. But then, who had?

"Dave, do you have a minute?" I asked. "I mean, I'd like to talk to you about something…"

"Sure. Come on back to the office."

I looked around Dave's jumbled wreck of an office, wondering where he and Paris had found the room to make out weeks earlier.

"I'm really sorry, Dave," I began, staring at the Woodstock poster on the wall. "I shouldn't have done that DNA test. It was really sneaky."

"It's okay. I'm glad you did. It was really courageous."

"It was?"

119

"I mean, you've really got your head screwed on straight, Brooke. You're not afraid to take on anything if you think it's the right thing to do."

I didn't know what to say.

"Maybe if I'd had some of your moxie when I was a kid, things would have been different. Maybe I could have spent my life with Denise instead of being alone."

"But, I thought you lost her phone number?"

Dave ran a hand through his thinning hair. "I lied. I knew where Denise was, but I was engaged to someone back in California. I meant to break up with her, but..." He held out his hands in a futile gesture. "She was already picking out bridesmaids dresses. And before I knew it, I was walking down the aisle."

I reached into my hobo purse. "Do you want this?" I asked, holding the World's Best Grandpa T-shirt out to him.

Dave looked at the gift. Tears filled his pale blue eyes. "Do you want me to wear it?"

"I do, but only if you really want to be part of our family."

He nodded, and began to sniffle. He hid his head in the soft cotton. Tears ran down my cheeks too. After a minute Dave looked up and held out his arms. Instinctively, I went into them, burying my head into his big bony chest.

"It's okay, honey," he told me. "Everything's going to be okay."

I have a grandpa now, I thought. *I finally have a grandfather*.

We cried a minute or two more, then Dave stood up and dried his eyes on the infamous T-shirt.

"Guess, I'll have to wash it," he said.

"Hand wash it in cold water," I said. "That way the letters won't run."

Dave rifled through a pile of junk on his desk until he found a pair of sunglasses. He put them on. Copycatting my grandfather, I put mine on too. Then he took my hand and together we walked out of Surf's Up into the sunny December afternoon.

Epilogue

Christmas vacation now over, it was almost a relief to go back to school. Somewhere I'd read that sometimes people who've been in prison commit crimes right away so they can go back into the slammer. They're scared. And, well, it's home.

Well, maybe Coral Cove High gossip would be positive for once. And if Sudsy was up to her usual blabber mouth mode, she'd probably told everyone about the Paris Breck arrest. I'd scoured Sunday's paper for any news, but obviously the police were waiting to cross all their t's and dot their i's before they broke the story.

Monday morning, I strolled through the front door of Coral Cove High, actually feeling cool and calm. Positive about life in general, I was ready to take on Paige Barton and her ladies in waiting. As usual, a crowd of popular kids stood in front of the trophy case. Paige and her entourage were conspicuously absent.

Instead I found Tamara and Sudsy, whispering away. They stopped when they saw me.

"Well, girl, it looks like you're a fashionista, after all," Tamara said, a big grin on her face.

"You mean my new Kate Spade hobo purse?"

Sudsy shook her head. "Something way cooler than that."

I barely had time to imagine what she meant but when who should come marching around the corner but Paige and her three BFFs. I stared, then stared again. Unbelievable! It couldn't be. Paige and company all had Joan of Arc haircuts and looked just like me!

Paige dispensed a mini-smile. Hi, Brooke," she cooed. "How was your Christmas?"

"Perfect," I answered. "How about yours?"

"Fabulous. As you can see, I've cut my hair too. I consulted with Charles, my hair stylist, and he went through all the latest magazines from Rome before he did it."

"Killer," I said.

"I know. We just love it. All we do in the morning is wash and mousse."

You'd think she'd just discovered how to split the atom. "I know. It makes life simpler, doesn't it?"

From then on, life did seem simpler. Tyler and I were back together. I had a new grandfather. And Paris Breck and her shoplifting gang were arrested and my name was cleared. Even Mrs. Ethos apologized and promised I could be in the Vocabulary Bee in the spring. I told her I'd think about it. I guess I realized that in life you don't have to win a prize to feel good about yourself. You can award yourself your own prizes everyday by just being you.

THE END

About the Author

LAURA KENNEDY lives in Tarpon Springs, a Greek sponge fishing town on the West Coast of Florida. She grew up in Minneapolis where her mother was a romance writer who helped her father support the family. By the time she was twenty-two, she lived in Southern California, was married, had a baby, and was broke, the perfect Petri dish for the beginning of a writing career. Encouraged by her mother's writing success, Laura borrowed her mother's portable typewriter on which she concocted her first story that sold for the staggering sum of $225.

Author Contact:
Blog: http://laurakennedy17.wordpress.com

Other Works by the author at Fire and Ice

Double-Take

CPSIA information can be obtained at www.ICGtesting.com
Printed in the USA
LVOW11s1530040616

491241LV00001B/18/P